TEMPTING CHASE

BURLAP AND BARBED WIRE #3

SHIRLEY PENICK

Photography by Jean Woodfin

Cover Models: Amanda Renee and Travis Keen

Cover design by Cassy Roop of Pink Ink Designs

❀ Created with Vellum

ABOUT THE AUTHOR

Contact me:
www.shirleypenick.com
www.facebook.com/ShirleyPenickAuthor

To sign up for Shirley's New Release Newsletter, send email to shirleypenick@outlook.com, subject newsletter.

About Shirley

What does a geeky math nerd know about writing romance?

That's a darn good question. As a former techy I've done everything from computer programming to international trainer. Prior to college I had lots of different jobs and activities that were so diverse, I was an anomaly.

None of that qualifies me for writing novels. But I have some darn good stories to tell and a lot of imagination.

I have lived in Colorado, Hawaii and currently Washington. Going from two states with 340 days of sun to a state with 340 days of clouds, I had to do something to perk me up. And that's when I started this new adventure called author. Joining the Romance Writers of America and two local chapters, helped me learn the craft quickly and has been a ton of fun.

My family consists of two grown children, their spouses,

two adorable grand-daughters, and one grand dog. My favorite activity is playing with my grand-daughters!

When the girls can't play with their amazing grand-mother, my interests are reading and writing, yay! I started reading at a young age with the Nancy Drew mysteries and have continued to be an avid reader my whole life. My favorite reading material is romance in most of the genres, but occasionally other stories creep into my to-be-read pile, I don't kick them out.

Some of the strange jobs I have held are a carnation grower's worker, a trap club puller, a pizza hut waitress, a software engineer, an international trainer, and a business program manager. I took welding, drafting and upholstery in high school, a long time ago when girls didn't take those classes, so I have an eclectic bunch of knowledge and experience.

And for something really unusual... I once had a raccoon as a pet.

Join with me as I tell my stories, weaving real tidbits from my life in with imaginary ones. You'll have to guess which is which. It will be a hoot.

To all the best friends out there.
The ones that went for it and the ones that didn't.

And to my own best friend and the many hours we spent riding
Mister Twister and standing in line to ride that roller coaster again
and again. Summer after summer.
Rest in Peace my friend, I miss you.

CHAPTER 1

*C*hase Kipling was glowering, he was furious and could feel it reflected on his face. The big family dinner with both his family and the Jefferson's had been fun, right up until his soon-to-be sister-in-law's brother started mouthing off. His dinner had been ruined and he'd just barely held it together until the ordeal was over.

His twin brother, Cade, looked at him with raised eyebrows. "What's got you so riled up?"

Chase huffed. He was certain his blood pressure was through the roof and he knew he needed to calm down before his head exploded. "Tim Jefferson going on and on about how sexy Katie is."

Cade shrugged. "She *is* a pretty little thing. It's hard for a man not to notice. Plus, she's such a sweetheart. I'm not at all surprised he thought she was attractive. Besides, he didn't go on and on, it was like one statement."

"Seemed like more than that to me," Chase growled. He'd wanted to punch Tim, so it must have been more than *one* comment. Katie was *his friend* and she didn't need some guy drooling over her. "I just don't like guys, especially tourists, ogling her."

"That's the most ridiculous thing I've ever heard. What in the hell is wrong with you? Are you jealous or something? She's been our best friend since... forever. Do you think no one else is ever going to think she's pretty? That she won't eventually find a guy and marry him?"

Jealous? Was he jealous? He didn't think so, but he sure didn't like what Tim had said. Was that jealousy or just protectiveness? Yeah, that's all it was, protectiveness. "Of course, guys are going to notice that she's beautiful. I only got upset because I'm protective of her."

Cade punched him in the shoulder. "It's not like Tim is an axe murderer or something. He's your soon-to-be sister-in-law's brother. And he seems like a nice enough guy to me."

"I still didn't like it. What if Rachel talks him into moving here and buying the mini-golf place?"

Cade shrugged. "So, what if she does? Although, I didn't get the idea he was really considering that. I think they were just thinking about fun ideas. Hell, you and I have talked about reopening it. Only because it's sitting there all sad and neglected. None of us really want to put in the time and effort to reopen it, we just don't like seeing it sitting there deteriorating. And I don't see Tim moving from Washington state all the way here to the mountains of Colorado to open a mini-golf place. Now stop acting like a dumb-ass and let's go. We still have to check on the animals and make sure they're bedded down for the night. It's our turn."

Chase sighed. "You're right, of course. I'm ready."

As Chase worked on his side of the barn, freshening water and adding hay to the feeders, he thought about his reaction to Tim's comments about Katie. What had gotten him so riled up in the first place? The facts—when he laid them out—were pretty simple. Katie is a good-looking woman. Tim is a nice guy, who lives in another state and has a life there. The mini-golf place does attract attention, but it would be a hell of a lot of work to open. Katie was his friend, his best friend, that he'd known since grade school. Men were going to look at her, and he couldn't get all pissed off every time one did. She was his friend, not his girlfriend or lover, just a friend.

By the time he'd finished with his chores he'd gotten his head back on straight. He hoped no one else had noticed his attitude earlier. He couldn't explain *to himself* why he'd been so out of sorts, and Cade had acted like he'd lost his mind, so he was going to chalk it up to…. Shit, he had no idea what to chalk it up too. Insanity, maybe?

KATIE JACKSON LOCKED the front door and turned the sign to closed. Another day, another dollar, as the saying went. It had been fun to see Rachel and Alyssa's brother Tim today when they had come in to gather the candy for the two families and the ranch hands. She still laughed every time one of the Kipling clan came in and walked out with huge bags of candy.

Every single person living on that ranch had an enormous sweet tooth, and whoever was going into town was required to bring back candy for everyone else. She always enjoyed watching the event. Some of them were quick and efficient, like Emma when she brought little Tony in. Surprisingly enough, Lloyd was also speedy, the first time he came in she'd thought he might have trouble because of his dyslexia, but he had no issues at all. Some of the others took forever, reading through each text and examining each shelf, looking for the exact item. It was amusing.

Rachel and Tim had been too busy chatting and goofing

around to be efficient. Tim was a flirt and had poured on the charm for her. She'd teased him back, but wasn't really interested. Although she did need to do something to move from where she was. Her heart was stubbornly holding on to hope that a certain Kipling would eventually see her as a woman instead of his childhood buddy. She'd turned that corner nearly ten years ago, and she'd been certain Chase would someday, too.

It didn't look like that was going to happen anytime soon. At least she had him as a best friend. A friend she hadn't seen in a week because they were all busy with the Jefferson's visit. Alyssa's college graduation was in a few days, and then maybe she could convince the twins into going to Karaoke, or possibly play to some cards. Bowling would be fine, too. Or even better she could talk them into taking her riding. They hadn't done that in a while and she thought getting on the back of one of their mares would be perfect.

She could call them and set it up for her next day off. The question was, which one should she call? Cade, since he was the most fun to talk to, or Chase, because she wanted to hear his voice? She sighed, what a fool she was, pining over a man who had her firmly in the 'friend zone'.

She finished her closing chores, and called Chase before she went upstairs.

"Yo, Katie. How ya doing?"

His deep voice sent a tingle through her body. Bad body. "Good, Chase. How are things at the Rockin' K?"

"Busy. Not to be mean, but I'll be glad when the Jefferson's head back to Washington."

"Me too, which is why I called. I have a hankering for a ride. When they all leave to go back to Washington, can I come to the ranch on my day off?"

"Of course. Cade and I would be happy to take you out on the horses."

"Next Wednesday?" she asked.

"You got it."

"Maybe I'll bring some cards and I can take your money afterwards."

Chase laughed. "You can try, darlin'. You can try."

"One of these days I am going to beat you, Chase Kipling."

"You keep trying Katie and the day you beat me you can pick any form of payment."

Katie shivered at some of the things she'd like to make him do. Kissing and nakedness popped into her head. She cleared her throat. "That's quite the incentive, Chase. You might regret that promise."

"I'll worry about that when I'm old and gray, because that's going to be when you finally do beat me. When I'm senile."

She laughed. "You never can tell when the winds of fate might change, Chase. Best not to tempt them."

"Not worried, Katie, you've got the worst luck of anyone I've ever played with."

She harrumphed. Her feet were tired, and she needed some food, so time to get moving. "Fine, gotta finish up closing. See you Wednesday."

"Cade and I'll be here waiting to take your pennies."

CHAPTER 2

*W*ednesday, the twins hurried through their morning chores. They had the day off as soon as they were done. Chase was looking forward to spending the day with Katie. She usually packed a lunch for all of them. They would ride for a while, probably into the National Forest. Then have lunch and afterwards head back to either his land or Cade's to hang out and play some cards.

They'd done those same things for years. When they were younger they would take a dip in the river or the beaver ponds. They didn't do that as often these days, but they could if Katie wanted to. They had swim trunks in their saddle-bags. No towels, so they would have to air dry, which is probably why they didn't do it nearly as much as they had as kids. It could get cold if the sun wasn't strong and hot. Youth didn't notice those kinds of things.

They'd just saddled the three horses when they heard a car pull into the drive.

Cade said, "Sounds like Katie is right on time."

"Yep, she's the one wanting to ride, so it figures she

wouldn't dawdle," Chase answered as he pulled the stirrup off the saddle to hang down.

They turned toward the door as Katie came into the barn. "I'm here!"

Cade laughed. "So, you are, we just finished with your horse."

"Oh goody. It seems like forever since we've gotten in a good ride. I brought lunch." She held out the food.

"Anything good?" Chase asked, trying to get a peek at what she had.

She hip bumped him. "Everything good, silly. So why are we standing here burning daylight? Let's ride, boys."

"Yes ma'am," the twins said in unison.

They led their horses out into the perfect late summer day. Katie chattered about work while they loaded enough food for probably six people into saddle bags. Chase was certain they would bring at least some of it back. Although not as much as a person would expect, because they did get hungry while they were out and about.

Katie looked pretty in her tank top and blue jeans that fit like skin. She had a jacket to tie onto her saddle, as did he and Cade. Colorado weather in the mountains could be unpredictable; hot one minute and hail or thunderstorms the next. He didn't see any clouds, so they would probably have a warm uneventful day, at least weather-wise. A day with Katie was never uneventful. The woman brought fun with her, wherever she went.

The leather creaked as Cade swung onto his horse. "So, any preference on direction, K?"

"Not really, let's give the horses a bit of a run across the pasture and then go into the National Forest for a bit. Maybe circle back and have lunch on the plateau."

"Not really, huh? Sounds pretty detailed to me." Chase shook his head.

Katie huffed and flipped her hair. "What would you suggest then, do you have a better idea?"

"Nope, just giving you a hard time. Lead on." He gestured for her to start moving.

"Fine, but try not to eat my dust." She let the horse know it was time for a run and took off, laughing all the way.

Chase and Cade grinned at each other and were off like a shot.

Chase loved to watch that woman ride, she rode like she was born for it, but rather than hang back and watch, he let his horse catch up to her. Cade had done the same, riding on her other side. She gave them both a happy smile and they all slowed so they didn't tire the horses out too early on their adventure.

SPENDING the day out in the sunshine on the back of a horse with her two best friends was just exactly what Katie needed. She was content and happy. And if her heart yearned for a bit more from Chase, it was just going to have to long, because there was no way she would jeopardize the friendship she had with him and his brother for the uncertainty of romance. Because that's all romance was, it was uncertain and fleeting, whereas friendship was strong and steady and lasted. The three of them had been friends for nearly twenty years.

Not one relationship, for any of them, had lasted more than a few months. She didn't really count the one Cade was kind of in now, because it had nothing to recommend it. That was simply a mean, nasty woman taking advantage of Cade's laid back, easy going nature. Tanya Fielding was a sneaky snake and the fact that Cade put up with her at all was a miracle, plain and simple. Katie hoped, someday, that he would find a nice woman to date.

Katie couldn't stand to be around at the same time Tanya was, she wanted to punch Tanya and strangle Cade. So, she made sure to make herself scarce when Tanya was going to be around.

They stopped for their picnic on the plateau overlooking the ranch. The land spread out before them, vast and treeless until right along the river where there was an abundance of aspen, cottonwood and pine trees. Most of the land had hay and barley growing to feed the horses in the winter. But some of the pastures had native grasses and that was where the cattle were currently grazing. The Rocky Mountains ringed the area on three sides and you could just barely catch a glimpse of the lakes in the distance. It was beautiful. A whiff of wood smoke carried on the air and Katie wondered if it was from someone cooking their lunch in the National Forest.

"Geez, Katie, do you think you brought enough lunch? There are only three of us." Cade was unloading the saddle bags with Katie, while Chase made sure the animals were in an area where they could eat some grass, too.

Katie tried to keep her mind on her tasks, but she liked to watch the way Chase moved. She caught herself glancing in his direction where he tended the horses, more often than she should.

Katie said, "I hear you talking Cade. We'll see how much we actually take back with us. The apples are for the horses."

Cade stood there with a mouthful of apple from the one he'd bitten into. He looked at the apple and then at the horses and back at the apple, shrugged and swallowed. Looking sadly at the apple, he said, "Oh, well, one of them will have to share."

Katie laughed. "Gotcha. I brought four, since I know you love apples."

Chase walked up and nudged her. He had a sparkle in his

eye that showed he knew her tricks and was just barely keeping his laugh from bursting forth. "Doesn't he do this every time you bring lunch?"

Katie thrilled that he knew her so well. She grinned back at Chase. "Yep, pretty much."

"That's just mean, Katie." Cade shook his finger at her and she grabbed it.

"Nope, you're just that easy."

Chase laughed and nodded. He tossed his brother the other apples. "Dumbasses have to pay, take the other three apples over to give to the horses."

Cade muttered as he took the apples over and gave one to each animal. Chase and Katie grinned at each other and Katie wished he would kiss her or something, anything. Instead she handed him a plate and started loading food on her own.

They were about finished with lunch and munching on the homemade cookies she'd baked when Cade's phone rang. He looked at it and groaned. "It's Tanya." He punched answer. "Hey, babe."

Tanya's loud voice spewed out of the phone. Cade cringed. "It was spur of the moment. Just hanging out with Katie and my brother. Not a planned outing or day off."

Katie winced, thinking now Cade was really going to be in trouble. From the screeching coming from Cade's phone, she was right in that assessment. Cade turned red and walked off a few feet, but his voice carried on the wind. "Now Tanya honey, you know Chase and I have been friends with Katie our whole lives."

Katie turned to Chase. "Maybe we should pack up the picnic. It appears that Cade is going to be dealing with some things. Some cranky things."

Chase nodded. "Yep, you're right. Sounds like a good idea."

"I don't want her to join us, do you?" Katie stuffed the leftover fruit and cookies into the saddle bags, they'd eaten all the sandwiches and chips, so she tucked the empty wrappers into another pocket.

"Hell no, not even when she's being nice, and that is clearly not the case today." Chase shook out the blanket removing crumbs from the picnic plus dirt and grass from the plateau, then rolled it to tie it on his saddle. "We can encourage him to go make nice and we'll go in the opposite direction."

She would be perfectly happy alone with Chase for a while, she just wished he would take advantage of their solitude, but she knew he wouldn't even think of it. "Excellent plan."

They got the horses ready, then waited a few more minutes while Cade argued with his girlfriend. It was terribly awkward, and Katie felt bad for him.

She heard him say, "I'm coming down now," before he shoved his phone in his pocket and stomped over to them. "Sorry about that. I'm going to have to cut the day short, while I talk to Tanya. Sorry to bug out on you K, but drama calls."

"No worries Cade, I hope I didn't cause you any trouble."

"Not you darlin', it's all her. Maybe it's time to move on. I'm getting tired of her *and* her bullshit. I'll see you guys later." Katie felt bad for him but could only hope he carried through on his words, that woman was poison.

Chase said. "Good luck, brother."

Cade climbed on his horse and was gone in no time.

Chase shook his head. "That woman is a pain in the backside. I hope someday he does realize that and moves on. It would be good for him to be with someone I can stand to be in the same room with."

Katie nodded. "Glad to hear it's not just me that has issues with her."

Chase shook his head. "Not even close to the only one. Want to head down to the river? Give the horses a drink?"

"Absolutely, we don't have to let her ruin our day, but I do feel bad for Cade." She looked back the way Cade had gone.

Chase shrugged. "His choice."

As they took the opposite path down the mountain from the one Cade had taken, she wondered if it was true that it was his choice. There were times that she felt like she could do nothing but love Chase. Did she have a choice in the matter? Could she move on? She should work on that idea. She didn't think she could ever love someone as toxic as Tanya was though. She just couldn't imagine it.

CHAPTER 3

$\mathcal{C}$ hase and Katie rode the long way around to his land, so they didn't bump into Cade and Tanya. If Cade had taken her to his designated piece of the Rockin' K ranch to "talk", Chase didn't want to get any closer. Since Chase's plot was further away from the main house than Cade's, he felt safe that they wouldn't come any further out than Cade's portion.

By the time they got there the horses were tired and thirsty. He was happy to pull their saddles off and let them have a rest. There was plenty of grass and water for them to drink. He felt a swell of pride to look at the land he would eventually build a house on. It was a good section along the river.

Chase was feeling hot too, and the water looked so refreshing. Katie was gazing longingly at the river and he couldn't blame her. "Want to take a dip? It's late enough in the summer that the water shouldn't be too cold. Do you have your suit?"

"I do, and that does sound nice. It was a hot ride going the long way to avoid Cade." She glanced around, then said quietly, "And Tanya."

"Yeah, it was. Go change in the girl bushes and I'll change in the boy bushes." When they were young they had designated the different sides of his land with bushes for changing clothes.

It still made him smile to think of themselves back then. They'd run tame on the ranch, playing out in the fresh air and sunshine, knowing they had to be back before it got dark. Sometimes Katie would spend the night and all of them would play hide and seek in the evening for hours. Occasionally their parents or some of the hired hands would join in the fun, and they would have a bonfire to roast hotdogs and marshmallows. It was a good way to grow up. He hoped, if and when he had kids, they would do the same and not be glued to electronic devices.

Chase stripped out of his clothes and pulled on his swim trunks. He tossed his clothes down onto his saddle as he walked toward the river. He had a nice calm inlet, that was just deep enough to swim around in, where some rocks blocked off the rushing of the river. He waded in and sank down, so the water would cover him. It was chilly, but not freezing.

As Chase waited for Katie, Tim Jefferson's words about her returned. He still didn't like it, but he'd never really thought about Katie in terms of her being a woman. She was his best friend, plain and simple. Was she hot? Maybe she was, but he'd never thought of her that way. He'd pay attention when she came out of the bushes and into the water.

Dolly, his brother's pet cow, ambled into the area just as Katie came out of the bushes, and he was damned glad too, because it gave him a moment to get his equilibrium back. The woman who'd just walked out of the changing area was not just hot, she was smoking hot.

She went over and was talking to Dolly, giving her a rub and scratch behind her ears like you would a dog. Katie had on a neon purple one-piece swimsuit. It was cut high on the hips and low in front and had nearly no back at all. She wasn't tall, but she was built like a goddess, curves in all the right places. How in the hell had he never noticed, in all the years they'd been friends, that she was gorgeous?

She kissed Dolly on the nose and as she bent to do so, he had a fine view of her ass. He groaned to himself at the delectable sight and tried to distract himself. Her long hair was pulled up in a ponytail, it was brown on top with the ends turning a golden color. He didn't think of her as having blond hair, so he wondered if she'd colored it.

She turned and gave him a huge smile. She had a wide mouth, made for kissing, with high cheek bones and large finger dimples on both sides of her mouth. Her brown eyes sparkled with mirth, under arched eyebrows. "Dolly came to play."

She was speaking to him and he had to respond, but he was too confused and lustful to think. He cleared his throat. "Yeah, I see that."

She laughed, gave Dolly one last rub and walked over to join him in the not nearly cold enough river.

"Is that a new suit?" he asked, casting around in his mind for something to say to get his mind off the sexy woman joining him for a swim. The sexy woman, who fifteen minutes earlier, had been his best friend. He wasn't sure he would be able to stuff her back into that box, now that his eyes had been opened. But he was damn well going to try, and succeed, even if it killed him.

"Nope, it's nearly as old as we are. But I still love it. You can't find this color much these days, so I keep wearing it."

"It's nearly fluorescent."

"That's why I love it." She dove into the water and he felt

her brush up against him, right before his legs were yanked out from under him and he fell backwards into the river. As his head slid below the surface, the lust was pushed away, and the water fight was on.

KATIE WONDERED why Chase was acting all stiff and weird. If she hadn't been completely convinced that he would never look at her that way, she would have sworn he was looking at her with desire. Sexual desire even. But that was ridiculous. They were friends. He'd never even looked at her with appreciation, let alone anything nearing lust. It must have been wishful thinking on her part. When she'd walked out into the clearing and seen him all wet with his muscles glistening in the sun, she'd nearly melted into a puddle of want.

She'd never been so happy to see a cow in her life, especially Dolly, since she could love up on the bovine while she fought to get her emotions under control. Then she'd turned around and seen the look on Chase's face, and she was hot and bothered all over again.

She was damn well not going to make an ass out of herself, by reading anything into it, so starting a swimming war was just the thing she needed. The water was wonderful, not too hot and not too cold, exactly the right temperature to be refreshing. She felt bad again for Cade to be missing out and wondered how his talk with Tanya was going.

She didn't have long to think about Tanya and Cade, as Chase came up from behind her, lifted her into the air and threw her into the water. She barely had time to draw and hold her breath before plunging into the cold depths. She stayed submerged deciding about her next plan of attack. She swam around behind Chase and then pushed off the smooth rocks below, to launch herself onto his back.

She didn't have the strength to push him down, he was a head taller than she was, and outweighed her by seventy-five or even a hundred pounds, but she was determined to do something. What she was going to do, she didn't know.

He laughed at her feeble attempts. "I seem to have a monkey on my back. A wet squirmy monkey." He leaned back and disengaged her arms, so she fell back into the water. She let go with her legs and floated away with a small kick off his ass to propel her along.

They played in the water for a while longer until the cold started seeping into their bones, then they got out and sat on the picnic blanket, so they could dry off enough to put on their clothes. They munched on the fruit and cookies leftover from their lunch.

Chase asked, "So what are you working on?"

She knew he was referring to the home crafts she made and sold on the internet. "I just finished a string art project for an author. It's a peacock feather. It took me some time to design the pattern, but I think it turned out great. Want to see?"

She got up and retrieved her phone out of her jeans, so she could show him. He'd always been very supportive of her hobby. She did all kinds of kitschy decorator crafts; string art was just one of them. The most popular was wine racks. She had several different designs people could pick from and then she would personalize them with their name or a favorite saying.

She showed him her most recent project and he made approving male grunting noises, which from him was high praise.

When they were mostly dry they pulled on their clothes and saddled the horses. Katie got the blanket and rolled it up to give to Chase. Before she could hand it to him, Dolly bumped into her back propelling her into his arms. He caught her and then looked into her eyes as the air became charged. He looked at her mouth, then back into her eyes. Her breath backed up in her lungs. She was sure he was going to kiss her.

Disappointment and relief warred in her body and mind, when he pushed her back, making sure she was steady on her feet again. They both looked at Dolly, who almost seemed to shake her head at them and amble away.

Katie laughed nervously, thrust the blanket into his hands and went over to mount her own horse. When Chase was on his horse she didn't look at him. She said, "Race you." Then wheeled her horse around and took off toward the house.

CHASE DIDN'T KNOW what in the hell had just happened. One minute they were getting the horses ready to ride back, and the next minute Katie was in his arms and looking at him with such a sweet look. She smelled like heaven, like sunshine and river and Katie. He'd wanted to kiss her wide luscious mouth and had almost done so, before his brain reengaged itself and reminded him she was his buddy, his pal, his best friend, and to kiss her would destroy those things. He'd freaked out and practically shoved her away. He'd seen a flair of something in her eyes, but he had no idea what it had been. He wasn't sure he even wanted to know.

As he raced back to the house he put that pulse of desire and the accompanying terror into a locked cage in his mind, never to be opened again. He couldn't bear to lose her as a friend, so he wasn't willing to act on the desire he felt. Damn Tim Jefferson, for putting ideas into his head.

CHAPTER 4

*K*atie was excited to be attending Beau and Alyssa's wedding. It was a perfect day for it. The skies were clear and blue, but the temperature was not too hot. At the bridal shower she'd heard that Alyssa's favorite color was red, so she was wearing her short red dress. It hit her mid-thigh and had long sleeves. It wasn't skin tight, but it did fit her like a glove. She decided to wear her knee-high leather boots, because they made her feel powerful and sexy, at the same time.

She'd locked up the store and put the sign she'd made in the window that said they were closed for a wedding and would reopen tomorrow. If someone needed something they would have to drive into Granby. This was the first marriage in the Kipling family for this generation, and she was certain the entire town would be there to celebrate.

Katie reapplied her lipstick, fluffed her hair and was ready to go. The church was just down the street and the reception was at the Grange, just one street over, so she would walk. With the parking in town as it was, she probably wouldn't get any closer than the store anyway.

She'd dropped off her gift at the ranch earlier this week. It was a string art design for Beau and Alyssa's future house. They were just starting to build on the land that had been designated as Beau's. The gift had their first initials in a heart, with their last name below it. It would look great over a fireplace or a door.

Katie walked down the street to the church and noticed a lot of people were milling around. Some were townspeople she'd known all her life, and others were strangers that she assumed were from Alyssa's home town in eastern Washington. Nervousness settled in her belly as she caught the eye of several men. She wasn't normally someone that attracted attention. She knew she was pretty enough, but nothing spectacular. Then again, nearly everyone she saw on a daily basis was someone she'd known all her life, and even when it was tourists she was always dressed in work clothes. So, she supposed her red dress had something to do with the attention.

She looked around for someone to go stand with and was thankful to find Summer, whose family ran the feed store. Summer looked relieved to have Katie join her. Katie had seen Tanya with Cade and figured their discussion the other day had been smoothed over, since they were together today.

Summer smiled. "Thanks for coming over here. I was feeling a little out of sorts. The only woman I recognized was Tanya, and you know how she and I get along. Who are all these people?"

Katie shrugged. "I assume people from Washington. Alyssa said their town was smaller than ours, but I'm finding that hard to believe with so many coming here."

"They must have closed down the town and rolled up the sidewalks," Summer said with a grin.

"Well, hello ladies." Katie looked up into the eyes of Tim, Alyssa's brother.

"Hi, Tim. Do you know my friend Summer?"

"I can't say that I have been introduced to this lovely lady. Hello, Summer. I'm Tim Jefferson, one of Alyssa's older brothers."

Summer held out her hand. "Nice to meet you, Tim."

He took her hand and brought it to his lips. "The pleasure is all mine, I can assure you."

Katie rolled her eyes at him. "You are such a flirt."

Tim tried to look wounded, but his eyes sparkled. "Only when such lovely ladies are present."

A girl about twelve years old came up. "Tim, mama says to quit your flirting and come into the church. You need to get a flower pinned on you or something like that. Even though you aren't actually in the wedding, mama says you need to have a flower because you're family. See, I got one too, but it's on my wrist with a bracelet thing, since I'm singing a song."

Tim looked chagrined, told Summer and Katie he would see them later, and went off with his sister.

Katie and Summer grinned at each other and decided to go into the church to get a seat. This group was going to pack the place.

CHASE WAS SURPRISED at the number of people that had driven for two days to attend his brother's wedding. Alyssa must have been popular in her home town, which didn't really surprise him, she was friendly and outgoing. Not that his town hadn't shown up in droves, but they didn't have to drive for two days either.

He'd heard some people had also flown into Denver and rented a car. There was an old woman, that had to be pushing ninety, who walked in on the arm of one of the men about his age. He hoped they had flown, two days in the car was a long time for an older person to sit, but she looked like a lively woman, there was nothing fragile about her. She was petite, but her demeanor belied her size. He was curious to know more about the tiny dynamo. When he got a chance, he would ask Rachel or Alyssa about her.

The wedding had looked perfect to him. No one fell down or passed out. He'd helped usher, as had the rest of his brothers and some of Alyssa's. Alyssa and Beau had chosen two attendants only, because if they'd included the siblings from both families it would have taken an hour to get them all down the aisle. Plus, both families were stacked on the male side, so they would have had to recruit lots of women to pair them up.

Alyssa's sister, Beth, had opted to sing a song rather than be an attendant. She had a lovely pure voice for a teenaged girl. It was an excellent decision in his opinion.

The reception was being held at the Grange Hall and they'd all come over yesterday to help with the setup and decorations. Alyssa and Beau had chosen to let the church and Grange ladies do the cooking and serving. The Rockin' K ranch had supplied all the beef, so that just left the side dishes. They'd been thrilled to provide those, and Chase noticed his favorite fruit salad was being served, the one with the tiny marshmallows in it. Score!

Chase filled a plate and wandered the room. It was packed with people, congratulating the bride and groom, and eating and drinking. They had a local band set up in the corner and there would be dancing once all the people had eaten.

A woman from Alyssa's home town had driven in early to make the wedding cake, and the church had been happy to let her use their commercial kitchen. It looked like a masterpiece to him. He'd never seen anything quite so elaborate. It was almost a shame to cut it up, but he'd heard one of the layers was chocolate with raspberry filling. He hadn't even known a wedding cake could have different flavors, he thought they were always just white cake with frosting in between. Alyssa and Beau had picked out three or four different kinds of cake with various fillings. He'd also heard one was going to be a spice cake and another was lemon, both sounded tasty, but he didn't want to make a pig out of himself. Maybe they would leave the leftovers, and he could sample the other flavors.

When the dancing started Chase noticed Katie was being passed around like a piece of meat. But as he watched closer he could see all the women were going from partner to partner, and for that matter so were the men. It didn't seem to depend on which town they were from, everyone was dancing with everyone else, even the old lady.

He decided to get a few dances in himself. He danced with some of the women he knew and also some he didn't. His most memorable partner was the older woman he'd noticed earlier. She'd marched right up to him and told him it was his turn. Introduced herself as Mrs. Erickson and then she'd grilled him. Question after question about who he was, what he did for a living, what his hobbies were, and what kind of grades he'd gotten in school, especially third grade. But her last question was the killer.

"So young man did you and your twin brother over there, with that woman barely letting him breathe, attempt to trick your teachers?" Mrs. Erickson asked.

He tried to hedge because of course they had, he didn't think they'd ever been too successful at it, but they had tried.

She glowered at him. "It's a simple, yes or no question. Spit it out, I'm not getting any younger."

"Yes, ma'am we did try to trick our teachers every once in a while."

"Good, no twin set worth its salt hasn't tried. I don't imagine you were terribly successful at it though. The two of you have completely different demeanors. Maybe if you tried it in the first week with a new teacher from out of town. But beyond that it wouldn't work at all."

"Really? I thought we were often confusing to people."

"Only clueless people. Just like you are, dear boy. Now walk me back to my table I need a small rest before I go pry your brother away from that cling wrap in the short dress."

Chase laughed and escorted her back to the table she was sitting at. And he didn't wonder about the clueless remark until the Washington contingency had left the area.

Mostly because he was distracted by Katie dancing with other men. He noticed that Tim was dancing with her over and over. He tried to ignore that and enjoy himself but every time he saw the two of them dancing again it notched his temper up.

Finally, when he couldn't stand it any longer he went over and cut in on Tim. "You've had more than your fair share with Katie, Tim. It's my turn."

Tim had the panache to grin at him and swoop some other woman up in his arms.

Chase looked at Katie's surprised expression and growled. "You've been dancing with him all night, I was beginning to think you two were joined at the hip."

Katie rolled her eyes at him. "Don't be ridiculous. I think I've danced with every man in here, except for you and Cade. Tanya seems to have her nails sunk in deep tonight. I don't think she's let Cade dance with anyone but herself. Poor guy. You've been out with a lot of ladies yourself. Any of those Washington women catch your eye?"

Chase was surprised by her question. He'd been so focused on who Katie was dancing with he had barely noticed his partners. He was, however, noticing Katie, she felt so good in his arms and she smelled like heaven. "Not really. The most interesting was the old woman, I gather she was the third-grade teacher in their town. She intends to dance with Cade and if anyone can get him away from Tanya it will be her. The other women seemed nice enough."

"Yeah it feels like our town folks and their people are nearly interchangeable. I can see why Alyssa feels right at home here."

Thinking of Alyssa moving here reminded him of Rachel teasing Tim about buying the miniature golf place. Chase thought about the idea of Tim moving to their town and didn't like it one bit. Even worse would be if Katie moved to Washington. That would really piss him off. Although he didn't agree at all, he grunted some reply that she would take as agreement. He didn't want them to be interchangeable.

CHAPTER 5

*K*atie grinned when Chase walked into the drug store her family had owned for generations. "So, it's your turn for the candy run, is it?"

Chase groaned. "It's not my fault. I need some blades for my razor and I made the mistake of actually mentioning that fact near a family member. Not five minutes later I had twenty texts with candy orders."

"With your beard I don't imagine your razor gets much of a workout. The last time you bought blades was probably when we were still in high school." Katie laughed. "I'm sure your big, bad self is capable of buying a little candy for your family and ranch hands."

"I'm not sure of that at all. In fact, I'm not sure my truck will hold it all, I might need to rent a trailer," Chase whined. "I could just tell them you were closed today,"

She wagged her finger at him. "Oh no you don't. Your family and their collective sweet tooth keep us from going under when all the tourists head home to avoid the weather and before ski season starts. Now stop whining and get to your list."

Chase sighed like she'd just sentenced him to death row. The man was quite the drama queen at times. She chuckled and pointed him to the candy aisle. He glanced at the aisle then turned back to her.

She pointed again. "You might want one of the carts to help you carry it all," she said sweetly.

"You are an evil woman, Katie Jackson, and here I thought we were friends."

"Since first grade, Chase. Now quit stalling and get after it."

As he went about selecting all the candy on his list, he thought back to Tim dancing with Katie at the wedding. He'd been jealous as hell and had cut in on them after Tim had danced with her over and over. He'd been kind of a dick and he needed to apologize to Katie, she hadn't deserved his wrath.

He'd been worried that Rachel's hinting about Tim buying the old mini-golf place was more than just a pie in the sky idea. What if he was considering it because of his attraction to Katie? But Tim had loaded up in his truck and driven off with the rest of the family after the wedding, so he decided she was safe. He had to wonder why he felt that way, Tim was a nice guy with good morals, so it wasn't Tim exactly. He just didn't really like the idea of anyone hitting on Katie. He'd gone to claim a dance with her when he couldn't stand watching any longer and had been abrupt with her. He needed to find a way to make sure she wasn't pissed at him.

He shook his head and tried to concentrate on his purchases. Fortunately, the store had small grocery carts to use so he wasn't trying to carry it all and read the list on his phone. Katie finished ringing up another customer and then came over to join him.

"You seem to be taking forever, have you never bought the family candy before?"

"Sure, I have, but my mind wandered for a minute and then I had to figure out where I was on the list."

"That's right, you are a man, and cannot even pretend to multitask. I would offer to help you, but it looks like I have another customer that might really need my help." She bumped him with her hip and sauntered off.

Maybe she wasn't pissed. She was acting like her normal self. Tim was right. She was a fine-looking woman, and now that his eyes were opened he could see that. She was on the short side and had a killer figure. Nice ass, good tits, small waist. Her eyes were a dark brown and her hair hit her waist in back. She'd done something to the ends to make them blond rather than the medium brown that was her natural color and it hung down her back in soft curls. Yep she was a gorgeous woman, Chase could see why Tim was attracted to her. But he better not lay a hand on her or Chase might be compelled to deck him. She was still his best friend.

And he should really apologize, she was his best friend and he owed her that much. He also needed to get his own self under control, looking at Katie as something other than his best friend was wreaking havoc on his mind and body. Maybe he should have decked Tim on principle.

KATIE HELPED her customer who was looking for maps of the area, both the National Park and the National Forest. She glanced over to see Chase sigh and put his phone away. He must have completed his candy buying. Now if his guy brain would remember what he actually came to her store to buy, that would be a miracle.

Almost as big of a miracle as if the man across the store were to look at her like the woman she'd become, rather than the little girl that had been his buddy. She sighed, that was never going to happen. She'd hoped he would since they were juniors in high school when she'd first seen him as a man. That had been ten long years ago and it just wasn't happening. She really needed to move on, because it was frustrating the hell out of her and she didn't know how long her heart could handle the futile yearning. But there had never been another guy that even piqued her interest, and that just sucked.

Tim Jefferson had kind of hit on her during the wedding and she'd enjoyed flirting a little, but he wasn't Chase. When Chase had cut in on her and Tim she'd thought maybe there was some jealousy going on there, but she'd talked herself out of that idea when she'd tried to flirt with him and he didn't notice.

When Tim had loaded up his truck and driven off she hadn't even felt a twinge of regret. Which kind of pissed her off, she was twenty-seven for goodness sake. She would like to get married and have a family someday. But she didn't even know where to begin to look for a man.

They lived in a small town and sure there were tourists in the spring and summer, hunters in the fall, and skiers in the winter. Nearly every one of those people came into her store. But so far, no one had sparked her interest at all, not one tiny spark, except for the man rummaging around in the shaving section. She sighed and went to go see if he needed help.

"What are you looking for?"

"Blades for my razor."

"In the shaving section, really? I'm not sure that's where

you should be looking, Chase. Idiot. I know you're looking for blades. Can you be a bit more specific?"

"Last time I bought them, they were in a blue package."

"Chase, the color of the package is irrelevant. What kind of razor do you have? Single blade, double blade?" The man just stood there blinking at her. She put her hands on her hips, could he be more obtuse? "The kind that snap on with double or triple blades? Or the old-fashioned kind that open up and you put the blade inside?"

"Oh, they snap on."

"Good. Any idea what brand? They aren't always inter-changeable."

He ran his hand down his face. "No."

Oh, for goodness sake, she couldn't remember him ever being quite this stupid. What was wrong with him? "Maybe you should just buy a nice electric razor. You're only shaving your neck and keeping the rest trimmed."

He rubbed his neck, which drew her attention to it and she wanted to shave him, slowly and then kiss the freshly smoothed area.

He said, "Show me what you've got in mind that would work for both."

She shook herself out of the fantasy and took him over to show him what his options were.

When she finally got the man rung up and out the door she was ready for a drink, or a nap. He was not normally an idiot, if she didn't know him so well she'd have been convinced otherwise. Not only was he being particularly clueless, but he seemed distracted. She wondered what was on his mind.

CHAPTER 6

𝒞hase was glad to finally get out of Katie's drug store. He'd never been so confused in his life. After he'd gotten all the candy in the basket and she'd come to help him in the shaving aisle, his mind had gone down a path he didn't like.

He'd started fantasizing about her. Stripping her down and taking her every way he could think of, in her own store. That had made all the blood leave his brain to head south and he hadn't been able to think, at all. And he'd panicked at the idea he was thinking of her that way. What in the hell was wrong with him?

Now that he was away from her, and his wild ideas, his body was starting to relax. He knew exactly what kind of razor he had, and what kind of blades it took. But when she'd come up to him and asked, he couldn't remember shit, not even his own name.

So, now he had a brand new electric shaver, which he didn't want. And no blades for his real razor. Hell itself would freeze over before he went back into her store, however, so he would just have to use the electric. He could order the blades online or drive to Granby.

Once his mind had gotten started down the path of lust he hadn't been able to think of anything else. This was craziness and he didn't know what to do to stop it. He wished it was just a case of horniness, but it was not. This obsession seemed to be focused on Katie and Katie alone. If he thought he could divert it with another woman he would do so in an instant. But he didn't feel desire for any other women.

Maybe if he didn't see her for a few days he would get over it and go back to normal. Yeah, he would try that. And dammit he still hadn't apologized for his behavior at the wedding.

KATIE HADN'T HEARD from Chase or Cade in a week and she was bored. She wanted to see them. She'd been busy all week with lots of tourists during the day, and in the evenings with a wine rack someone had ordered online. But the wine rack was done, it was Friday night and she wanted to go out. Maybe she could talk them into Karaoke or bowling. She decided to call Cade this time since she'd called Chase last time. She also wanted to find out if they would be stuck with Tanya if they went out, because washing her hair would be more fun than that.

Cade answered on the first ring. "Katie, to what do I owe the pleasure of your call?"

"I was wondering what you guys are doing tonight."

"I am celebrating the fact that Tanya is in Steamboat Springs with her mother for the weekend. What did you have in mind?"

Thank goodness Tanya was out of town, now she could

have a fun night without worrying about trouble. "A night on the town, Karaoke, or bowling?"

"That would be most excellent. Let's do Karaoke, we've been haying, so my body would prefer sitting on my ass, instead of throwing a heavy ball around."

She laughed. "Very good, we wouldn't want your arm to give out and you to drop the ball on your toe."

"The way I'm feeling at the moment that's a likely scenario. After I shower I might be better. I'm certain Chase will be happy to go along with that plan. He needs to get out, he's been grumpy this week. No idea why, he won't talk about it. Tanya's been around a lot, so that might be all it is. He doesn't care for her much. I can't blame him, she can be difficult."

Katie wanted to say something snarky but held her tongue. "Want to meet there? Say eight-ish?"

"Sounds like a plan. See you soon."

CHASE STOOD at the bar waiting for his turn to buy some beers for him and his brother and a margarita for Katie. Next to him a couple of guys going on and on about some hot woman. God save him from drunken tourists.

The bartender, George, said, "You guys are going to have to slow down a bit or order some food. You've been going strong for three hours now."

"Man, you aren't my mother," one of the drunks said, "I can drink whatever I want."

George replied, "I'm not your mother, but I can cut you off if I feel you are unsafe."

The other drunk said, "Fuck that, it's only eight and we ain't driving anywhere we're staying in that shit hole around the corner."

Chase winced, knowing the inn they were referring to was run by George's family, as was this bar.

"That may be true, but you still must either order some food or have a soda to dilute the whiskey a bit. The soda is on the house." George was doing a great job at controlling his feelings, Chase wasn't sure he would do as good of a job.

Drunk number one waved his hand. "We don't need your fucking charity. We need another shot, asshole."

George shook his head. "I'm sorry, sir."

Drunk number one flipped off George and pushed his glass onto the floor. "Fuck you. Fine, we'll go find our fun somewhere else."

"Let's go find that little honey we saw this morning and have some fun with her," drunk number two said.

Chase didn't like the sound of what the men were saying. These two seemed to be kind of nasty drinkers and he felt pity for any woman that would be with them

Drunk jerk one said, "Naw, she wasn't into us."

"Who cares, we can convince her," drunk jerk two said, "she just needs a little persuasion."

The two assholes stood and started lurching toward the door. Chase felt a chill run over him and asked George, "Do you know who they were talking about?"

George shook his head. "Nope, I don't think they knew her name."

A woman on the other side from where the men had been sitting said, "They kept talking about the general store and the little gal who ran that."

Chase snapped his gaze to the woman. "The grocery store or the drug store?"

"Definitely the drug store."

Fear coursed through his body and he looked at George. "Tell Cade and call Drew or the police."

Then he ran out the door like his hair was on fire. Katie

34

should be walking down to the bar at this very moment and if those assholes found her first... he couldn't even go there.

Chase flew down the street looking for the drunks or Katie. He heard a scuffle in the alley and ran into it, to see his worst nightmare.

Katie was shoved up against the wall and both men were manhandling her.

He saw red. Roared. And charged them.

Yanking the first one off of her, Chase knocked him flat with one punch. The second one she kneed, and he bent forward where Chase delivered a solid blow that felled him completely.

He turned to Katie and gathered her into his arms. "Are you okay? Did they hurt you?"

She gulped back tears. "No, you had perfect timing. I couldn't get enough room to fight back."

"I know, sweetheart," he held her and rocked her. "When I realized what they had in mind my heart stopped, I was so terrified."

Katie looked up at him and he couldn't do anything but kiss her. He had to make sure she was going to be okay. It was meant to be a small touch, but it grew into a conflagration instantly. Her taste was exquisite. Her mouth warm and welcoming. He was lost in the moment until he heard Cade yelling their names. They jerked apart, and he called out to his twin.

Cade rounded the corner and pulled Katie into his arms. "Are you okay, K-girl?"

"Yes. Chase got here at the exact moment I needed him to."

"Thank God. The Sheriff's department is on the way to lock these two clowns up, for the rest of their natural lives, if I have anything to say about it. We'll have to go to the station and tell them what happened."

Katie nodded. "I think this has effectively ended our night out. After I talk to the Sheriff, I think I'll just go home and soak in the tub. I feel kind of dirty."

Chase's heart broke at her expression and he wanted to grab those two men and pummel them until there was nothing left but goo on the street.

She came over to him and took his hand. "You scraped your knuckles."

"It's nothing. You're the only one important here."

Cade said, "I'm going to go out in the street to direct the law in here."

One of the guys groaned and Chase turned on him, ready to kick the shit out of him.

Katie grabbed his arm. "It's okay. It's over. They aren't going to hurt me."

He turned back to her and put his forehead to hers. "I've never felt fear like that in my life. Not riding bulls. Not in lightning storms. Not even when I got lost as a little kid. Or that time my foot got caught when we were diving into the river and I thought I might drown. My fear of them hurting you far surpassed everything."

"I'm fine. Thank you."

"Aw, Katie. I'd do anything for you girl, you're my best friend."

She pulled away. "I know, Chase, but I can appreciate you getting here at exactly the right moment, anyway. Here comes Drake and both your brothers."

Chase was relieved to see Drake, the Sheriff, was on duty tonight, it would be easier to work with him than one of the deputies. And his brother, Drew, was also working tonight, so he knew they would be extra thorough gathering evidence, knowing it was Katie who'd been attacked. Drew was already the most persnickety person he knew when it came to his job, but Katie was dear to all of them, so there would be no stone left unturned.

They spent the next hour at the Sheriff's office giving their statements to Drake. Drew had gone back to the bar and talked to the bartender, the woman who was still there and a couple of others that had observed the drunk men. Drew and the Sheriff thought the men might end up with some jail time, since they'd been spouting off about Katie for hours while they got drunker and drunker.

Chase and Cade drove Katie home after the ordeal and Cade walked her upstairs to make sure she got in her door safe and sound. Chase was still feeling shaky from all the adrenaline that had coursed through his body. Once they got home they both had a strong shot of whiskey, to decompress, and collapsed in bed. It had been one hell of a night.

CHAPTER 7

*K*atie went directly to the bathroom, she started a hot bath and poured some salts into the water. She was going to soak until she got pruny. When those men had attacked her, she'd been terrified, and she'd known they were bent on sex, with or without her consent. They'd come into her store earlier that day and had been trying to flirt with her, but she'd ignored their crude attempts to engage her and had been professional with them. They'd said something as they left about her being frigid, so she already knew they were not nice men.

Later she'd been in a hurry to meet up with the twins, so she hadn't been paying any attention to the people on the street. When the men had grabbed her, and dragged her into the alley, she'd been too shocked to respond until they shoved her up against the wall. By the time she realized she was actually in danger from them, she didn't have any room to maneuver, but she wasn't going to go down without a fight.

The jeans and cowboy boots she'd worn tonight had given her protection that the dress she'd been thinking about wearing would not have, so that had been in her favor. Of course, Chase roaring around the corner and decking that one guy had given her the opportunity to knee the other one. She was thankful he'd heard the two assholes and had followed them, she shuddered to think what might have happened if he hadn't been standing at the bar when George had cut them off.

She slid down into the water and winced, she was going to have some bruises tomorrow, but it was a small price to pay for escaping those two.

Leaning back in the tub she closed her eyes as the hot water relaxed her. Her mind drifted back to the kiss. It had been magnificent, the best kiss she'd ever had. Too short, but then again Cade coming in and finding them locked in a hot embrace, would have been extremely embarrassing. They would have ended up being the town gossip for weeks. She smiled thinking about the Bonnie Raitt song and giving the whole town something to talk about.

But then Chase had ruined the whole thing by saying she was his best friend. Not that she didn't love being his best friend, but being a little more than his best friend would be even better. However, she wasn't going to jeopardize what she did have for what was essentially pie in the sky.

The warm, fragrant water calmed her nerves and soothed her body, so she soaked until the water started to cool, then she scrubbed her skin until it was rosy, sending all her negative feelings swirling in the water draining from the tub. She noticed some bruising already starting on her arms as she pulled on flannel pajamas. It was kind of hot for flannel, but she wanted the comfort. She could turn on a fan to stay cool.

Knowing Chase as she did, she sent him a text. Then she climbed into bed and was relieved when she drifted off to sleep easily.

～

CHASE WAS WIDE AWAKE. He'd dozed for a few minutes when he first laid down, the alcohol helping to relax him. But then he'd started thinking about what might have happened to Katie if he hadn't been standing by the bar and his mind whirled with dire scenarios, among them rape, murder, kidnapping. He was making himself crazy with all the possibilities.

He forced himself to remember she was a strong woman for such a tiny thing and she would have fought them tooth and nail, and quite possibly have been able to take care of herself. Two on one, made that more difficult, but if anyone could have fought them off it would be Katie. When he'd distracted the men, she hadn't hesitated to fight back. He chuckled thinking that one guy wasn't going to be walking straight for a few days.

He'd been so relieved he'd kissed her right on the mouth, and now that he thought about it she'd kissed him right back. So, what did that mean? Was she simply expressing her joy in being safe again? Did she mean it as something more than that, and for that matter did he? It had been a delicious kiss, warm and welcoming, her scent and taste mingling together in his senses, drawing him into her. If his brother hadn't called their names he didn't know what would have happened. He'd definitely been on board and if he recalled correctly she'd rubbed up against him in an invitation for more.

But then later she'd pulled back from him and there was nothing left of the sensual woman from the kiss. He couldn't remember why she'd pulled back, or exactly when it had happened. He supposed anyone who had gone through what she had, would close herself off some afterward.

Which led him to start thinking about how thankful he

was he'd heard those two drunks talking and that the woman at the bar had paid attention. Those thoughts went back to what might have happened had the circumstances been different, if he'd chosen the other end of the bar, or if they'd let the waitress take their order.

His mind circled back to the dire possibilities again. Around and around in a loop it went. His mind whirling a mile a minute through all the stages of the evening, again and again, when his phone chimed an incoming text.

Katie: I'm fine. Go to sleep!

He laughed, she knew him better than anyone. The tension and anxiety left him, flowing away like a cooling river. He relaxed and felt his mind settle, she was fine, he'd been there when he needed to be. He texted her back.

Chase: Yes, ma'am.

And he did as she had directed, he fell asleep, knowing everything would be fine.

CHAPTER 8

*K*atie woke with a start. Her heart pounding, her thoughts confused. What had woken her? Was it a noise, or a dream? She listened carefully not daring to breathe or move. Eyes wide open searching the darkness. She heard nothing, sensed nothing. Too afraid to check the time on her phone, if she looked it could illuminate her and if someone was there, in the dark, they would see her and she wouldn't be able to see them.

She lay there not moving, barely breathing for several minutes. But as nothing stirred, slowly her body began to relax. Finally, she did reach for her phone to check the time, four in the morning, ugh. Too early to get up, but could she get back to sleep? She didn't need to get up for at least a couple of hours yet.

Katie willed her body to relax, one muscle at a time. One thought at a time she forced her mind to think calming thoughts. Until she drifted back off to sleep.

When Katie woke again the sun was just coming over the mountains. Her room was bathed in the soft glow of morning. She thought back to the events of last night and realized she was at peace with them. She wondered what had awoken her in the early morning and thought maybe it had been a stray animal or even the paper carrier getting an early start to go out fishing. It was supposed to be a pretty, warm, late summer day.

She hummed as she got dressed, and only winced a little at the bruises that had formed on her arms and various other places. As she pulled on a shirt, she felt a big one on her back where they had shoved her up against the wall. It might not hurt to take a painkiller with her, in case she got sore during the day. She got her travel-sized container and shoved it in her jeans pocket.

In the kitchen, she put a bagel into the toaster and looked out toward the lake. With the living quarters above the store, it made her viewpoint just high enough to skim over the top of the buildings behind her and give her a small slice of the lake and the mountains beyond it. After slathering her bagel with cream cheese, she took it and a glass of orange juice to the table to eat.

She was one of those weird people who didn't like coffee. It tasted burnt to her. Maybe she'd just never gotten a good brand, but she hadn't tried very hard to find some she liked. Water was her primary drink of choice, with some juice in the morning and a margarita if she went out on the town.

She'd been looking forward to a margarita last night. Those guys had screwed up her whole plan, assholes. Well, she'd just have to talk the guys into it another night but finding one where Cade could come without Tanya would be a challenge. She sighed and wished either Tanya would suddenly become a nice person or that Cade would get a clue and move on.

The one good thing about the whole evening was the delicious kiss from Chase. Unfortunately, that taste only made her want another, and she didn't think that was going to happen. The kiss had been a tension reliever more than anything. Not as much on her part since she'd been waiting for him to kiss her for ten years. But she was certain that's all it had been on his part, a release of adrenaline and possibly confirmation that she was really fine. She knew Chase loved her, there was no question about that, but the unfortunate part was that it was a brotherly love, dammit.

She finished her bagel and downed her orange juice, rinsing the glass in the sink and then putting it and her plate in the dishwasher. After filling her thermos with ice and water she went out the back door, locked it and skipped down the stairs around to the front door. Where she stopped dead in her tracks.

One of the big picture windows at the front of her store was shattered, some of the glass still held in place by the molding. It looked like a scene from a horror flick. Now she knew what had woken her in the night. She pulled the phone out of her pocket and called the Sheriff's office.

After she'd told the dispatcher all she could see from her viewpoint and assured her she would not go inside or touch anything, she took a picture of the window and sent it in a text to the twins, with a caption of "the fun continues". Both of them texted her back that they would be there as soon as their truck could get there.

She sat on the stairs leading up to the front of her store and waited.

CHASE MET his brother in the hall, both of them pulling on clothes as they rushed through the house. When they got to the kitchen they told their sister, Emma, that Katie needed them, and could she spread the word that they would be back as soon as they could. Emma agreed, and they hustled out to get into Cade's truck, since his was the closest to the door.

As he finished buttoning his shirt, Chase said, "What the fuck. Do you think the window has something to do with last night?"

Cade slammed the truck into drive and peeled out of the driveway, leaving a cloud of dust behind. "I don't know how it could, Drake said they would be locked up until mid-morning at the earliest."

Glad he'd already shaved, showered and brushed his teeth, Chase finger combed his hair. His hair was still wet, although not drippingly so. He glanced at his twin and noticed he hadn't gotten around to a shower yet that morning. Score one for the early bird. They had some chores in the morning, but most of their work for the day would be later toward mid-day and afternoon. It was a weekend, but work on a cattle ranch didn't cease, it just slowed down some. That allowed his brother a few extra minutes of sleep. Cade was not a morning person, Chase didn't mind early as much as his brother, so he was usually up and moving quicker.

Cade screeched around a corner. "She won't be able to get a piece of glass that big today, we'll have to get her some plywood to put over it."

"You're probably right, we could check to see if anything is open in Grand Junction. But that large a sheet of glass would probably have to come on a special transport truck. We can't just throw that in the bed of the truck."

"No, and I think that large of a window would best be replaced by a professional."

"Didn't think of that, but you've got a point." Chase held on as Cade whipped around another turn that would lead them into town. "You better slow down, no need to run over kids and dogs, Katie isn't in danger, after all."

Cade braked to slow the truck. "Don't need a ticket, either. Although they should be at Katie's. Not looking for speeders."

"True, but let's not tempt fate. It's not been on our side the last twelve hours."

"That's for damn sure." Cade sighed. "Although things could have been worse."

Chase shuddered at the thought. "Don't remind me."

They pulled up in front of Katie's store and saw her talking to one of the deputies, while another one was up next to the window looking at the evidence. Chase hopped out of the truck and went to stand beside her. She reached for his hand and he held on tight to her cold fingers to give her moral support while she answered the man's questions.

Cade went over to where the other officer was examining the window.

The deputy said to Katie, "So let me make sure I got the facts straight. You woke up about four AM?"

Katie shifted from foot to foot. "Yes, a little before four, because I laid there listening for a while before I looked at the time. I startled awake, so I didn't want to move until I could figure out if there was any danger."

"So, does sometime between three-thirty and four sound about right?"

"Yes."

"But you don't recall actually hearing anything?" He asked.

"No. I was sound asleep and then I was awake and fearful. You know, heart pounding scared."

"But you never went to investigate?"

"No, when I didn't hear anything, I just went back to sleep."

The deputy put the pencil behind his ear. "Okay then. We'll do some more investigation in the store, it will take us about a half hour if you want to grab a cup of coffee. Then you can look to see if anything was stolen. You'll probably want to put some plywood over the window until you can get the glass people out here."

Katie nodded to the deputy and then looked at Chase.

Chase said, "Of course, we'll help you with that."

"Thanks." She smiled weakly at him.

He squeezed her hand. "Do you want to stay here or go across the street to the café for a cup of coffee? Or upstairs?"

"Let's go across the street. I want to sit down and let someone else make the coffee."

Chase nodded. "I am capable of making coffee or tea for you, if you don't want to be around people."

"Thanks, but being with people is fine and I could use a donut or something. I had a bagel earlier, but I've used that all up, freaking out and talking to the Sheriff's department, telling them the same thing over and over and over."

"Just making sure they got the facts straight. At least it wasn't Drew, you know how relentless he can be."

She finally gave him a nearly full smile. "I do and I'm glad he was on last night instead when it was more serious. The deputy said those guys are still in jail, so they couldn't have done this."

Chase signaled to his brother that they were going to the coffee shop. "I figured they would still be in jail. No one would rush in to deal with guys that harass women."

"But if it isn't them, who could it be?" She sighed like the whole world was on her shoulders. "We've never had anything like this happen before. Not since I've been old enough to know about it anyway."

Chase held the door open to the café, so she could go in before him. "I have no idea. Just let the police handle it. Hopefully someone saw something."

She didn't look convinced. Jen came up to take them to a table. "Looks like you've had some trouble, Katie. Hi, Chase."

"Yeah, I don't want to, but I suppose we should sit where we can see the building and what the lawmen are doing." Katie shrugged and seemed to shrink before his eyes.

"You got it hon. Follow me. Is Cade going to join you?"

Chase was so busy worrying about Katie he barely heard her, he shook his head to clear his thoughts. "It's hard to say with him. Give us a four top just in case."

Jen said, "I'll bring you coffee, Chase. Katie, do you want water or something else?"

Katie looked so sad he wanted to hold her on his lap and rock her. "I think some hot chocolate. Comfort food, you know."

"Of course, I'll be right back."

Chase took Katie's hand to give her strength or comfort or just someone to hold on to. He didn't really know what to say or how to help, but he could hold her hand.

KATIE WAS SO glad Chase was with her, he wasn't saying much, but just knowing he was beside her, helped her to be strong. Kept her from spiraling into depression or hysteria. He was her anchor while she was feeling storm-tossed and confused.

Jen came back with their drinks. "Do either of you want food?"

Chase said, "Yes please, your big breakfast. I hadn't eaten yet when Katie texted us."

Katie saw Cade walking across the street. "Cade is coming."

"Two of them then, Jen. Cade hasn't eaten either."

Jen nodded. "What about you, Katie?"

48

She thought some protein might be a good idea, rather than a donut, it looked like she was going to need it. Plus, the hot chocolate was enough sugar. "Maybe some scrambled eggs and wheat toast."

"With a little cheese like you like it?"

Katie nodded.

Jen said, "I'll get this order put in and bring Cade back some coffee."

Cade rushed in the door and over to their table, flinging himself into the chair. "Did you order me food? I'm starving."

"Of course," Chase told his twin. "So?"

Cade leaned forward. "It looks like someone whacked it with a hammer or something, there wasn't a rock or anything else inside that would break a window. But the guys didn't think it looked like anyone went inside. The glass didn't look disturbed, even. There were jagged pieces coming up from the bottom, so it would have been hard to climb over those since the window ledge is a good three feet up."

Katie didn't know what to think about that, her chest tightened and there was a flutter in her stomach at the idea of malicious damage. "Someone just smashed my window for no reason? Just to be mean?"

Cade nodded. "That's what they think anyway, they're going to go inside and look around some more, but from the outside that's their conclusion."

"But why would anyone do that? I don't understand." She gripped Chase's hand tighter.

Chase ran his thumb across the back of her hand and over her knuckles in soothing circles.

Cade shrugged. "No clue, K. But Chase and I will get some plywood to put up over the window for you. You probably can't get glass before next week. Do you want to open today? No one would blame you if you didn't."

Did she want to open? She didn't want to just go sit in her

apartment with nothing to do and the twins probably had to get back to the ranch. Cade had mentioned they were working on the hay this week. She might as well open, after she cleaned up the glass, that is. "Yeah, I might as well. I need to clean up the glass first." She sighed. "The plywood will look ugly, but it's necessary."

Chase said, "It doesn't take two of us to buy a sheet of plywood. I'll stay and help you with the glass."

She felt relief at his statement and wondered why she was feeling anxious about cleaning up the mess. She smiled weakly at Chase. "Thanks, I could use the help."

Cade was watching her and then turned to look at his brother. She wondered what silent twin communication was happening at that moment. Cade nodded and said, "True, I can manage to go to the hardware slash feed store alone. Do we need anything for the ranch while I'm there? Never mind, I'll call dad. I've got tools in my truck, so once I get the wood, we can put it up."

They finished their breakfast and went back across the street. Katie hadn't noticed when he'd gotten there but Sheriff Drake had arrived at some point while they were across the street.

He walked out of her store and came over to the three of them. "Katie, you're welcome back in the store. It doesn't look like anyone entered it, but look around and see if anything is missing, just in case."

She nodded her agreement.

Drake looked at the twins. "You two going to give her a hand?"

Cade said, "Yes sir, I'm going to get some plywood and Chase is going to help her with the glass cleanup."

"Good. This looks like someone just being mean. It could be kids. It could be random. But based on what happened last night I have to wonder if it was a coincidence. I don't believe in coincidence, but those guys from last night are still locked up in my jail with pretty heavy hangovers, so I have no way to link the events. I'll keep my eyes open and you do the same, Katie."

"I will, Sheriff." She felt her throat closing with tears and needed to get off the street. "Thanks, can I go inside now?"

"You sure can. I've got the dimensions for the window. I'll give them to Cade."

She hurried inside before she broke down in the middle of the street. Chase stayed right beside her, but she noticed him look back toward his twin and the Sheriff.

CHAPTER 9

*C*hase wondered what Drake was telling Cade. Drake was their father's best friend and had always been a fixture in their lives. He was acting a little strange and clearly was talking to Cade about whatever he suspected.

He'd find out later. Katie was his first priority and she was looking a little fragile. He followed her to the back room where she just stopped. Looking around like she was confused.

"Are you all right?" he asked.

She looked up at him with tears in her eyes and shook her head. "No, Chase. I'm not."

As silent tears tracked down her face, he pulled her into his arms. Tucking her head under his chin, he held her tight while she cried. His heart broke at her distress. If he had any words of comfort he would voice them, but he had nothing, nothing at all, so he just held her.

After a few minutes she looked up with a watery smile. "Thanks, I needed that."

"Happy to be of service."

"Thanks for not telling me everything is okay, or any of the other trite things people say."

She was thanking him for being a dumbass and not trying to help? He could deal with that. She didn't have to know his mind had not held any thoughts, at all. Not one single thought.

Chase ran one hand down her arm. "Sure, ready to get that mess cleaned up? I can get started if you want to… wash your face or something."

"I'll do that. The broom and dust pan are in the closet and there's a big trashcan up front under the counter. I emptied it last night before leaving for Karaoke. Was it really just last night? It seems like it's been a week."

He nodded. "Yeah, just last night, but a lot has happened since you took the trash out."

"Isn't that the truth. I'll be out in a minute."

Carrying the broom and dustpan to the front of the store he looked the window over from the inside. More glass was going to fall as he pulled the big pieces from the window. He swept up what was there, but knew he wasn't finished with that job yet. Grabbing a pair of heavy-duty gloves Katie had for sale he pulled them on, so he could start on the jagged pieces of glass. Drake's appraisal seemed spot on, that no one came inside, there was way too much glass still stuck to crawl in the window.

The plywood they would nail up would detract from the looks of the building. If it was going to be up for a while it would be worth it to do something with the surface. Maybe paint it or… hey he could get some markers or paint and draw a cute picture on the front of it. He did pretty good caricatures of people, he could do a depiction of the towns-folks. Katie always did like his drawings, and it might cheer her up.

He could probably come over after work today. As he

cleaned up the glass he thought about the idea and a picture started to form in his head. When Katie joined him, he had to fight the grin that wanted to break across his face, at the plan he'd concocted to decorate the wood.

"I've got the glass, you look around and make sure nothing's missing. I agree with Drake, I don't think anyone could have gotten in here, but you should still check to make sure."

She looked at him oddly and then nodded. "I'll check, if you don't need any help."

"Nope. Put these gloves on the Rockin' K's tab."

"But…"

"No arguing, I'll take them and put them to good use, don't you worry. I needed a new pair anyway." He didn't really, but it was a good excuse.

Once he got all the glass cleaned up he didn't know what to do with himself while he waited for Cade. He tried not to think about the kiss last night. It had been magnificent, but he kept reminding himself it had happened because they were both relieved that she was safe, and no harm had come to her. But he had to admit he felt even more protective of her since the kiss, and he wouldn't mind another one or twenty. No. She was his buddy, his pal, his best friend, nothing more.

He decided he could do some shopping while he waited, he still needed blades for his razor and he could see what she had for art supplies for her plywood. He had some things at home, but the plywood probably would be very absorbent with a rough finish, so he wasn't sure if what he had at home would do it. Markers might be good or possibly pastels. Pastels might actually be the best because they wouldn't absorb like a marker would and possibly fade.

Cade came in and found him in the art supplies aisle. "What are you doing? I thought you were helping Katie. Not buying toys."

Chase saw Katie was helping a customer that had come in. "I am. She's so bummed out about the ugly plywood covering the window I thought I could surprise her by drawing a caricature on it of the townspeople."

A slow grin slid across Cade's face. "That is an excellent idea. I talked to dad to see if we needed anything from the feedstore and told him what happened. He said if Katie needed support and some protection today one of us could stay with her. Since you actually came up with an idea to make her smile. You can stay, and I'll go back to work."

"Really? I planned to work on it tonight after work."

Cade glanced toward Katie. She was still busy with a customer. "Drake doesn't want her by herself for a few days. He can put an extra watch on the store, but he wants her to have someone around just in case."

Chase saw Katie start their way. "Got it. Here she comes."

"Are you two going to stand around all day yacking while birds and bugs fly into my store or are you going to put up the ugly plywood?"

Cade twirled her around in a pseudo dance move. "Why, little Katie darlin', we are going to put that ugly plywood up and keep them mean nasty critters out of your store."

Katie laughed, and Chase rolled his eyes at his brother. "All right Don Juan, let's get moving. Daylight's burning."

Chase turned to Katie and handed her the enormous pastel set he'd found on a bottom shelf and the razor blades he needed. "Ring these up please and I'll get them when we're finished hanging the plywood."

KATIE WATCHED the twins walk outside, their heads together. Something was up and since they had stopped talking about it when she walked up she knew it had to do with her. They would tell her about it eventually. They always did. But she'd learned during the many years that they would talk it through first. She'd also learned it didn't do a bit of good to try to cajole it out of them before they were ready. So, she would wait and be patient, even if it killed her.

Her phone chimed with an incoming text from Summer, not a surprise, since Cade had purchased the wood from her family's hardware store.

Summer: How are you doing? Cade told me about the window.

Katie: Sucks, big time. The glass people can't get here until Friday the week after next!

Summer: Oh man that's a long time to have a board instead of a window.

Katie: Right?! Fourteen days!!! It will make it dark in the store and ugly on the outside.

Summer: Some white paint would reflect, but that's a lot of work for a couple of weeks.

Katie: Yeah, so not worth it.

Summer: Maybe you could tack up a picture or a map or something.

Katie: Not a bad idea. I'll give it some thought. Thanks.

Summer: Let me know if I can help.

Katie: Will do. TTYL. Customer.

Summer: Me too. Bye.

After she greeted one of the fishing regulars that came every year, she thought about Summer's suggestion. It might make her feel better to post something on the wood. They had a couple of tourist maps of the area that might be cute. And one of the National Park.

While her customer shopped, and the guys hammered, she went foraging for maps and a staple gun she knew was in the back room. The tourist rack had a town map that was not at all to scale but did show a whimsical depiction of the stores, lodging, and activities in the area.

It had a drawing of her store with its big picture window, she grinned when she put a tiny bandage over the window. She found a more technical map of the National Park, the one you automatically got when you paid at the entrance.

The town rodeo was in a few weeks, she'd seen some larger posters around town and wondered if they had any left. She'd put up fliers for it on her bulletin board, but had never had anywhere to put a large poster, well she did now, for two weeks anyway.

She rang up the sale for the fisherman, who wasn't much of a talker. He wasn't grumpy, just didn't talk much. "Thanks for coming in, good luck fishing."

The old guy saluted her and walked out the door, as the twins walked in.

"Plywood is up so no critters can get you." Cade looked at her closely. "I don't want to hear any complaining. Drake thinks one of us should stick around for a day or two, just in case. Chase is going to hang around today. We want you to come stay at the ranch tonight. Chase and I can bunk together, and you can have the other room."

Spend the night at the ranch? Drake was worried? Chase was staying? Her mind whirled with all Cade had dropped on her head. "But…."

Chase took her hand. "No buts, Katie. We want, no we need, to know you're safe. While Drake and the rest of them try to figure out what's going on."

"I already cleared Chase staying here today with dad. Emma is changing the sheets in Chase's room."

Katie couldn't think with Chase running his thumb over her knuckles, sending tingles up her arm. She had no idea how to combat the steamroller of the twins or their concern for her, with a heavy dose of Drake's warning on the side. Being safe was more important than arguing, when she really didn't mind and wasn't completely sure she would feel comfortable in her own bed tonight.

"Fine. But what will you do all day?" she asked Chase.

He picked up the package of oil pastels. "Pretty up your storefront. But no peeking until I'm done." He waggled his eyebrows at her.

She laughed at his silliness and felt some of the sadness drain from her as she wondered about what he would draw on the plywood. Spending the day near him wasn't a hardship. And the thought of sleeping in his bed made her blood heat. If he'd been planning to join her in that bed, it would be even better, but she would take what she could get.

"Okay, you win."

Cade grinned, and Chase sighed in what sounded like relief. They really *were* worried about her.

CHAPTER 10

*C*hase was thrilled that Katie had given in to Cade's plan easier than they had expected. They'd come into the store armed with every play they could think of, but they hadn't needed any of them. Which in Chase's opinion meant she was feeling more than a bit uncomfortable about being alone and sleeping in her apartment.

Chase sent his razor blades and the other things he'd picked up home with his brother, while he took the oil pastels and a pencil out to the front. He was content to be watching over Katie and making her something special at the same time. He could see both doors to the store, so no one could get past him without him knowing about it. The plywood didn't keep out all the sound, so he would be able to hear if she needed help.

As he drew he wondered about who might have broken her window and why. He couldn't think of a single person from town that would do something like this. They were a small enough population that they stuck together, even when they didn't like each other much. So, was it someone from out of town? Katie had said she'd had no run in with anyone except the men who were still cooling their heels in jail. It was certainly very strange.

He had the scene nearly drawn on the board with pencil when he heard the staple gun and felt the vibration in the plywood. He grinned and asked, "Whatcha doing, Katie?"

She was only slightly muffled. "Putting up some posters, so that bare board doesn't look so ugly. How is your picture coming along?"

"I've got it almost all drawn on. So, I can start filling in the colors."

"Oh goody. Let me know if you need some water or something."

"Will do. Want me to grab some sandwiches later at the café for lunch?" It was fun talking to her through the wall, like they were on a secret mission or something. He could imagine her expressions as they talked.

"Sure, whenever you get hungry. We can sit behind the counter and eat. I've got drinks and stuff to go with them. Or I could have the pharmacist watch the front of the store if you want to go across the street."

"No need, we can sit behind the counter. Like we did sometimes when we were little."

He could hear the smile in her voice when she answered. "Those were fun times. We felt so old being allowed back behind the counter."

"Yeah, good times." He saw a family of tourists start up the stairs to her store. "You've got customers on the way."

"Good, now get to work on my picture, I'm dying to see it."

He chuckled and took the sky-blue color out of the box. He would start at the top and work down the board, so he didn't smear what was already done. "Yes ma'am."

≈

KATIE WAS HAVING SO much fun with Chase being on the other side of the plywood. When she wasn't busy with customers or restocking the shelves, she would go back to putting up the posters and he would start chatting with her again.

He'd come in the store a few times to wash his hands or get a bottle of water or use the facilities. They'd had lunch behind the counter sitting on the ledge that was back there. He'd brought sandwiches and she'd supplied fruit, cookies and drinks.

It was mid-afternoon when she finally got all of her posters up. Chase's voice had sounded down further on the other side of the board, so she knew he was making progress.

Two young women in their late teens or early twenties came in giggling. They were tourists, so she went over to ask them if she could be of assistance.

"Yes, you can, you can tell us who that hunk outside drawing on the wall is."

"Yeah, the man has muscles on top of muscles. He might get mugged out there, with no shirt on."

Katie's brows went up. "No shirt? Really?"

"You didn't know? You have got to go take a peek, girl. You are missing one hell of a show."

"I'll be right back." She signaled to the pharmacist that she was going outside for a moment. He would keep an eye on the tourists.

Katie hustled to the door and about passed out when she saw Chase. He was squatting to work on the lower part of the board, and the girls were right, the man was magnificent. His back muscles gleamed and moved as he drew. He was tanned from the waist up from haying. It was a hot job so regardless of the dirt and scratchiness the men often worked in the fields shirtless. His nut-brown muscles bunched and stretched as he worked on the drawing.

He glanced over at her. "Hey, what are you doing out here. I said no peeking."

Katie shook her head. "You've got half the town watching you work shirtless, Chase."

"You're exaggerating. It was hot out here, I just grabbed what was handy when I got your text and it's too hot working next to pavement radiating heat."

Katie scanned the street where she saw several women on the big chairs and benches that sat on the porches most of the businesses had out front. "I count no fewer than twenty women watching the show."

Chase stood and looked around in surprise. "I had no idea." He grabbed his shirt and pulled it back on.

One of the women called out. "Katie Jackson, you are a spoilsport."

Katie chuckled, and Chase turned bright red. She whispered, "Own it, Chase."

He grinned at her then turned back to the street. "Show's over, ladies. Move along now."

One of the other shop owners hollered, "If I break my window will you come draw me a pretty picture, Kipling?"

"Nope. This is a gift to my girl."

Katie thrilled at the words, but then her brain kicked in and reminded her they were just friends. Bad brain. To take her mind off the disappointment of that idea she turned back to Chase as the women dispersed. "So, since I'm already out here, can I see it?"

"Sure, it's nearly done. I was just adding a few critters at the bottom."

She walked over to see the picture and was completely enthralled. He'd drawn a depiction of the town and the people who populated it. The lakes were down in one corner and the Rockin' K ranch was in the upper left one.

He'd drawn all his family up on the ranch except for

himself and his brother who were with Katie on the porch to the store. The twins were both loaded down with huge bags of candy, that had pieces falling out of them onto the ground.

He'd drawn Karen and the Singing River Ranch in another corner and the forth one had the road to the Rocky Mountain National Park in it. There was so much detail she knew she could look at it for hours and not see it all.

She whirled on him and grabbed him in a bear hug. "It's awesome, Chase."

"You like it?" he asked, sounding a little uncertain.

"No. I love it. When they put up the glass I'm going to have it mounted in my apartment. Thank you, thank you, thank you!"

"Just trying to cheer you up. Looks like it worked."

She dug her phone out of her pocket and took a picture of it. "Did you sign it? You have to sign it."

"Naw, it's just for fun."

She put her hands on her hips and tried to look fierce. "You have to sign it Chase. You've got room on that last little bit you were working on. Now do it."

"If you insist."

"I do. Now I'm going back in the store because those teenie-boppers that were drooling over you, have been in there alone long enough."

Chase grinned. "Teenie-boppers? I saw two college age girls go in your store right before you came out."

She poked him in the chest. "They are too young for you."

He rubbed his face like he was fighting a smile. "Oh, I don't know about that, we seem to be having a run of younger women marrying my brothers."

She poked him again. "Too young." Then she turned on her heel and went back in to see what the teenie-boppers were up to.

CHAPTER 11

*A*t the end of the day Chase and Katie drove to the ranch in her car. She'd packed up the essentials to spend the night and brought along a couple of bags of candy, since she knew what everyone purchased all the time it wasn't hard. Chase had tried to convince her it wasn't necessary, but she'd done it anyway.

When they pulled onto the ranch the entire family met them in the driveway.

Chase's mother, Meg, hugged her hard. "Don't you scare me like that again, Katie. My old heart can't take it. You're one of my own."

Katie's breath hitched at the sentiment, and she fought tears. "You'll never be old Meg, you've got too many kids and little Tony to keep in line."

Meg squeezed her again and passed her on to the next Kipling. By the time she'd gone through all the family, and had the stuffing squeezed out of her, she was near tears at the love and concern she felt from all of them.

Four-year-old Tony had whispered in her ear as he

hugged her. "I don't know why we're all hugging you, but I would never turn down the chance to hug the candy lady."

She smiled. "I would never turn down the chance to hug you either, Tony."

The ranch hands had heard the commotion and come out of the bunk house, so while everyone was assembled she handed out the candy she had brought with her. That made her even more popular than she had been, as each person thanked her for remembering them.

Finally, they went into the house. Chase had already taken her bag in, she assumed it was because he'd spent the day with her and didn't need to hug her one more time. Although she wouldn't have minded another hug from him.

They rehashed all the trouble and drama at dinner, being careful with their words so they didn't frighten Tony. No one had any idea who would do something like that, especially since they hadn't gotten in to steal anything.

Although Emma had stopped the conversation when she said that maybe they'd gotten scared off before they could get inside. That actually made the most sense of all. That it really was just a foiled burglary. Still not a good scenario but at least that wasn't personal. She'd been thinking all along that it was some kind of personal attack on her.

Emma's idea helped Katie to relax and she thought it would be nice to have a sister to talk things through with. Being an only child was not always fun.

After dinner some of them played penny ante poker and of course she lost, like she always did. She lost a whole whopping four dollars and thirteen cents and was glad they only played for pennies. Chase and Cade teased her about being the worst poker player ever and she vowed that someday she would beat them.

Cade grinned. "You've been saying that for twenty years, Katie girl."

Chase shook his head. "No. I don't think we started playing poker at the age of seven. I think she's only been saying it about fifteen years."

Cade nodded. "You're probably right. Mom wouldn't have let us play poker in elementary school. But we played Old Maid and Go Fish back then and she lost at those, too."

Chase smirked at his brother. "Ah yes, I forgot she was dreadful at those card games also."

"Standing right here while you malign my character."

"Not your character, just your card playing." Cade patted her on the head like a dog.

She growled and tried to bite him.

Chase pulled his brother back. "Now stop picking on Katie, she's had a hard day and can't help the fact that she sucks at cards."

Katie put her hands on her hips. "I'm going to bed; you two fools can stand around yucking it up at my expense without me having to hear it. Goodnight, boys."

She turned to walk out of the room.

Chase said, "We're just teasing you. If we didn't love you, we wouldn't tease you."

She held up her hand and kept walking. She wasn't really mad, but it didn't hurt them to think differently. In fact, it might be good for them. Idiots.

They dashed up next to her one on each side.

Cade put his arm around her shoulder. "You aren't really mad, are you?"

Chase wrapped his arm around her waist. "We didn't mean to hurt your feelings."

She relented and put her head on Cade's shoulder. "I'm not mad, but I am tired. It has been a heck of a twenty-four hours."

Both of them nodded at that.

Chase said, "We're relieved you're here with us tonight, so tomorrow can be better."

"Yeah, we're damned glad you're okay."

She swallowed. "Thanks for being there for me, guys. It means a lot."

Cade said softly. "We wouldn't have it any other way."

She put her arms around both of them as they walked down the hall to the bedrooms.

CHASE TURNED OVER AGAIN. He was comfortable enough on the blow-up mattress. He just couldn't get his mind off of the fact that Katie was asleep in his bed. It wasn't the first time she'd spent the night at their house by any stretch of the imagination. But it was the first time since he'd noticed how beautiful she was, and how much he desired her.

It was also the first time since the kiss, and she was in *his* bed. Not Emma's or Cade's, or on the couch, but *his,* and that was making him a little crazy. Fortunately, his nosy brother was sound asleep, or he would have questioned Chase's restlessness. Chase was normally the one who could fall asleep at the drop of a hat. Nearly standing up even. Not tonight though. Tonight, he was wide awake thinking about Katie right next door.

He had to stop this nonsense, she was his best friend, he had to work in the morning, he needed to go to sleep. Maybe a glass of milk would help. He'd heard milk had some kind of something that helped. Warm milk anyway. There was no way he was going to warm it up, that sounded disgusting unless it had lots of chocolate in it.

He got up and pulled on his jeans zipping them, but leaving them unbuttoned. He padded silently through the hall to the kitchen where he found the stove light on and Katie standing in front of it. He froze, not knowing whether to high-tail it back to the room, or stay there and enjoy the hell out of the shortie pajamas she had on. Her legs looked a million miles long even though she was barely over five feet tall. There was a hint of sexy curves under the top that made his mouth water. He should definitely leave. But before he could, she turned and saw him standing there so he walked in and noticed her catch her breath.

"It's just me."

"You didn't startle me, Chase."

"But I heard you gasp."

She nodded. "But not in fear."

He had no idea what she meant, she must have noticed because she turned back to the stove. "Never mind. Do you want some warm milk? I couldn't sleep, and it always helps."

"Warm milk sounds disgusting, without chocolate in it."

"No chocolate, but I did add some sugar and a touch of nutmeg. Try it, you might like it. I assume since you're up roaming around at one in the morning, you can't sleep either. And we both have to work in a few hours. I made plenty."

"Fine, you talked me into it."

She gave him a sly grin and reached up to get another mug out of the cupboard, which caused the tiny top to ride up and give him a glimpse of smooth skin above the tiny shorts. He bit back a groan and tried to look away. Not happening. He did manage to sit at the table without looking at the chair.

She brought the mugs to the table and slipped into the chair next to his. Close enough to smell, dammit. Was she trying to kill him? She smelled like heaven all warm and welcoming. He tried to distract himself with a gulp of milk, which was still too hot to drink, and it burned his mouth. He quickly swallowed so the fire could sear the rest of his insides.

Katie grimaced. "You might want to let it cool before you gulp it down."

"I did come to that realization, after I had a mouth full of scalding liquid. I thought you said warm milk not volcanic."

She giggled. "I usually let it cool a few minutes while I rinse out the pan, but you distracted me."

He shivered at the goose bumps that had broken out over his body at the sound of that giggle. "You distracted me too, which is why I didn't notice the steam pouring out of the cup of molten lava you call milk."

"Distracted you how? You knew I was in here."

He looked her up and down and she turned a delightful shade of pink.

"Oh. Well, you have no room to talk, mister."

He looked down at himself and his unbuttoned jeans and a slow grin moved across his face. So, he'd distracted her too. Now that was an interesting notion. He looked at her and he wondered if he really did see a bit of hunger in her gaze, before she looked back at her drink.

She lifted the cup to her mouth and took a tiny sip while he watched in thrall. She stared into her cup. "It should be cool enough to drink now."

He couldn't move. A horse whisper escaped him. "Katie?"

She shook her head. "Drink your milk, Chase. I think I'll take mine to my room."

As she fled out of the room. He said quietly, "My room." Then he drank the milk, rinsed out the cup and pan, while he thought about her reaction and what it might mean.

Katie was kicking herself as she rushed into Chase's room.

69

She'd freaked out when he'd looked at her as a woman. She'd been waiting for that moment for ten long years, and when he finally did, she'd rabbited. It had scared the crap out of her. Desire fought with fear. And fear of taking the next step had won.

Could she, should she, risk her lifelong friendship with him for a chance at something more? What if it failed, what if they tried it and it destroyed their relationship? Was it worth the uncertainty? The answer to those questions was not to be found.

She felt like such a fool.

Sitting frozen on his bed, she heard him walk down the hall. He paused at her door and she held her breath. Wanting him to come in. Fearing that he would. It seemed like hours that he stood outside her door as her heart beat a frantic tattoo. She didn't know whether to be relieved or disappointed when he continued down the hall to his brother's room.

Katie shivered as a chill settled over her. She finished her milk and crawled under the covers, certain she wouldn't be able to sleep, as she turned over the last few minutes in her mind.

But the milk worked as it always did, and she drifted off to sleep, to dream of possibilities.

In the morning she woke with it firmly decided, that it was worth the risk. And the next time she had the chance she would be brave and reach out for what she wanted. But that was not happening this morning, she had a store to run. He had a ranch to work.

Emma met her in the kitchen. "Tony and I are coming to town with you this morning."

"Emma, you don't need to do that. I'm sure you were right last night, and it was a foiled burglary, which means I'll be just fine."

"I'm coming with you, and we'll make sure that's true. If it is. I'll let Tony play in the park and I can keep an eye on your customers to make sure no one looks weird."

"And if they do?"

"I'll call the Sheriff," Emma said decisively.

"And if it's some tourist?"

Emma shrugged. "Drake can sort that out, or Drew."

Katie shook her head. "You all are being ridiculous. I'm sure I'll be fine."

"Better safe than sorry."

"Fine, but you'll bring Tony back here for his nap." She wasn't about to let Emma tire Tony out too much.

"If I feel confident you'll be safe, yes. If not, I'll put him down in your bed upstairs. That way I'll be within shouting distance."

Katie put her hands on her hips. "I still think you're being over-dramatic. And I plan to sleep in my own bed tonight."

Emma said, "We'll see."

CHAPTER 12

$\mathcal{K}$atie finally shooed Emma and Tony off in time for the little boy's nap. There were no more broken windows, and no one had been the least bit shady. There were plenty of tourists, as they were enjoying the last of summer. Lots of people were in the mountains to fish and camp and play on the lakes, one more time, before school started and the weather turned.

They would have a few more weekends of craziness after school began when the aspen turned golden. The contrast between the dark green of the evergreen trees and the yellow aspen was a sight to behold, so they would have lots of tourists on weekends until late September or early October.

She had a few weeks before she would start swapping out her fishing and camping gear for winter paraphernalia. Most of her store stayed the same because skiers still wanted to take back souvenirs, and the local population's needs didn't change that much. So, it wasn't a huge job and was in fact, kind of fun.

Katie was busy thinking about her winter plans when a

young girl walked in the door. She looked about ten or eleven and walked with hunched shoulders and her hair hanging in her face. Katie waited for someone to follow the girl in the store, but no one did. The girl wandered through the store for a few minutes before finally coming up to the counter with a few packages of cheese and crackers. She laid the snacks on the counter without looking at Katie and then dug up some money out of her pocket and laid it on the counter.

Katie smiled at the girl who was peeking at her through her hair. "Looks like you need a snack."

The girl gave a slight nod but didn't smile or speak.

Katie rang up the sale and told the girl how much it would be, then she counted out the amount of money the girl had pulled out of her pocket and noticed she was off by seventeen cents.

She told the girl, "You need another seventeen cents."

The girl's shoulders drooped, and her chin quivered. She started to push one of the packages to the side when Katie cleared her throat. "It's okay. You can keep it, I have some extra change that I can use."

The girl's head jerked up and she looked at Katie with wide eyes. Then she grabbed up the snacks and hurried out the door. Katie quickly followed the girl to the door to see where she was going. The girl had already torn open one of the packages and was eating like she hadn't eaten in days. Then she scurried between two buildings and was out of sight.

The rest of the day Katie wondered about the girl. She hadn't been very clean, her hair was dirty and stringy, there had been a smudge on her cheek and dirt under her nails. She hadn't looked familiar, so was she a tourist?

All kinds of questions went through her mind. Where

were her parents, was the first one. She would keep an eye out for the girl.

Drake came into the store at almost closing time. After exchanging pleasantries, he said, "So we discovered that your attackers have warrants out for their arrests. They won't be getting out of jail any time soon. In fact, several states are arguing about who has precedence. It seems those guys have been paving a path of destruction for a while. Everything from robbery to breaking and entering to disorderly conduct. Possibly even kidnapping. I haven't read through the whole list of offenses laid at their feet, yet. But you are safe from them. Any other trouble around here?"

Katie was relieved to hear they wouldn't be set free. She didn't realize she'd been worried about retaliation until the tension flowed out of her at his words. "Everything has been quiet. It must have been a fluke or an accident."

Drake nodded. "I'll keep an extra watch on the store and apartment anyway. I heard you don't plan to go out to the Rockin' K tonight."

Katie shrugged. "I don't think I need to. Do you?"

"You would be safer out there for sure, but I don't foresee any issues. Keep your eyes and ears open though and if something startles you, do not hesitate to call immediately. Understand?"

"Yes sir." Katie grinned at his attempt to be stern. She imagined he pulled it off just fine with strangers, but not so much with her or anyone that had always known him.

He saw her smile and huffed. "Gotta get going, you be careful."

"Don't worry I will. Thanks for letting me know."

She didn't think about the girl again until she was getting ready for bed. She wondered if she should have mentioned her to Drake. She would try to do so next time she saw him.

~

CHASE WAS both relieved and concerned when Emma told him that Katie was determined to stay in her own home tonight. He was relieved that she wouldn't be sleeping in his bed and causing him to think all kinds of crazy thoughts. He was also relieved that he wouldn't accidentally bump into her in the kitchen, with her skimpy pajamas just barely hiding her curves. But he was concerned that she wouldn't be safe in her apartment. His father had told him that Drake had called to say the men that had accosted her would not be getting out of jail, probably ever.

He'd texted her to make sure everything was okay, and she'd told him to stop being a mother hen and go to bed. That she would be fine and if she needed anything, she would call the Sheriff's department first and him second.

He didn't feel like he had anything else he could say to that, so he'd told her goodnight. Maybe they could get together on her day off, so he could make sure she was doing all right. He'd have to see what his father had planned for the day. He did have a job to do and while his dad was often accommodating, that didn't mean he could just do as he pleased, either.

He knocked on his brother's door from their adjoining bathrooms. He heard Cade grunt a welcome, so he walked in.

Cade looked up from his phone where he was obviously playing a game that he'd paused. "What's up?"

"Katie's staying at her house tonight."

"Pretty obvious, since she's not here."

"Just thinking, that we could possibly do something with her on her day off."

Cade shook his head. "No can do. I'm taking Tanya to Granby for dinner."

75

Chase felt his eyebrows raise. "To the steak and lobster place?"

"Yeah, she got pissed that we were hanging with Katie last Wednesday and then heard we'd been at the bar waiting for her on Friday. She's on a warpath, so I'm taking her out."

Chase didn't know what to say because he thought Cade should kick her to the curb. "I'll do something with her then. What time are we getting off that day, so you can shower, shave and kowtow?"

"I talked dad into early, seven to four thirtyish, but you don't have to work those hours if you want to work later."

"No that will be fine. I'll take Katie to a movie or something, get some dinner."

Cade frowned. "Don't go to that new super hero one. I want to see it too."

"You could take Tanya."

"Riiiight. When hell freezes over. You know she only likes sappy shit or overly dramatic, depressing, want to kill yourself movies."

Chase held in a "I keep telling you" comment and walked out the door.

He debated texting Katie to set something up for Wednesday, and then decided she probably was tired, since neither one of them had slept worth a shit last night. He had a couple of days, so he wouldn't disturb her tonight.

As he got ready for bed he thought about their encounter in the early morning, and wondered what would have happened if she hadn't run away. Or if he would have kissed her. He had no idea what might have transpired. Good or bad.

Thoughts were spinning in his head as he thought about the possibilities. When he crawled into bed a while later he realized that no one had changed the sheets from Katie sleeping in his bed last night. His whole bed smelled like her, especially the pillow. He groaned and couldn't decide if he wanted to get up and change them or bury his face in the pillow. Exhaustion hit him like a fist and he did neither, he gave into it, and dreamt of her.

CHAPTER 13

*W*ednesday finally rolled around and Chase had plans with Katie. He'd just barely managed to wait that long. He needed to make sure she was all right. They'd decided on dinner and a movie, but not in Granby where they could run into Tanya and Cade.

Dinner was Mexican, the hotter the better and margaritas to cool the burn. They passed food back and forth like they always did. Chase liked chimichangas and Katie wanted a ginormous burrito, plus they had to have nachos first, with all that dripping cheese and jalapenos.

Katie said, "My mouth is on fire."

"That's what the margarita is for."

"I drank it all." She looked sadly into her glass.

He fought the grin that wanted to take over his face. "Order another one."

She shook her head. "I won't be able to walk, and I will fall asleep in the movie."

"I'll poke you and wake you up, at least when you start snoring." He shoveled in another huge bite.

"I don't snore." She frowned at him.

He swallowed and shook his head. "I beg to differ. I've heard you snore on multiple occasions."

"I think it was Cade, not me. Or Emma, yeah Emma."

Chase grinned. "Are you going to blame it on the dog next?"

"I don't have a dog. And most of your dog's live outdoors, or in the barn. Except for that old yellow one that sleeps in the kitchen and he's too old to move."

"Maybe you could blame it on Dolly." He offered teasingly.

"That's not a bad idea, but I still don't believe I snore." She frowned. "That's not very lady-like."

He looked at her in her jeans and no makeup, she was a tomboy through and through, she was still a sexy little thing, but not at all lady-like. He thought he better throw her a bone, before she wacked him with something. "You snore softly and daintily."

She snorted. "Ow, I got hotness in my nose."

"No sinus problems for you, then." He tried to keep the smirk off his face and didn't think he succeeded.

She pointed her fork at him and tried to look fierce. "You are a pain in the butt, Chase Kipling."

He returned the gesture. "Right back at you, sweetheart. So, do you want another margarita? All that food will help soak up the alcohol."

"What a great excuse," she said tapping a finger to her bottom lip in thought.

He knew she wanted one, so he continued, "And the movie has too much action for you to fall asleep."

"And the walking?"

"I'll carry you if I have to."

"Ha! That would serve you right. Okay, you talked me into it."

He grinned at her while he signaled the waitress, Katie

was a little bit of a lightweight where liquor was involved, so two margaritas very well could put her out. They were having a lot of food though, so he wasn't worried. He could carry her if he needed to, she was such a little thing, physically anyway. Personality wise she was a giant.

She got a huge grin on her face when the waitress set the second margarita down in front of her and took a big slurp. He hoped he hadn't encouraged her to his, or her, detriment. But she tucked back into her burrito, so he relaxed.

Katie was having a blast with Chase at dinner, they'd only gone out together without Cade along once or twice. Cade being the more gregarious of the two normally carried the conversation, so it was interesting to have it be only Chase. He wasn't reticent at all, so she supposed it was just easier to let Cade run off at the mouth rather than try to get a word in edgewise.

She probably shouldn't be drinking a second margarita, but they were so tasty and cooling to the tongue. Even if she did get a little loopy, she knew she was perfectly safe with Chase, he would never let anything happen to her. She loved that she was both safe with him and could be herself. No fear of either danger or rejection.

She was happy she could be comfortable in her jeans and a flirty top. She'd slapped on some mascara and lip gloss and called it good. If she'd been going out with any other guy she would have obsessed over what to wear and put on real makeup. So, there was definitely something to be said for going out with a buddy. She wouldn't mind a kiss or two, but there were definite tradeoffs.

"So, want to try the Karaoke thing again on Friday?" she asked.

"Sure. I don't know what Cade will be up to."

She looked at the hot guy across the table from her and didn't miss his brother one bit. "We seem to be doing fine without him."

He grinned. "We are, aren't we. I guess we don't have to always be the three musketeers."

"Nope, but if he wants to come that's cool, too."

His grin dimmed a little. "Of course."

"I'm getting full. What time is the movie?"

"We've got about forty-five minutes."

"Good. I think I'll get this boxed up for tomorrow and we can drop it by my house on the way to the theater."

"We can do that."

When they stood to leave she felt a definite kick from the alcohol, but it wasn't too bad, she hoped. She made it to his truck and clambered up into it, thinking it seemed a lot higher off the ground than it normally was.

When he pulled into the alley at the back of her building near the stairs to her apartment, and then volunteered to run her food up, she didn't argue, but thankfully handed him the keys. While he was gone she leaned her head back against the seat and watched the darkness through slitted eyes. She saw movement down the alley a bit and sat up straighter. It looked like someone was by the dumpster of their little grocery store. She didn't move, just sat and watched. When Chase came bounding down the stairs she saw the figure scurry off. Something was familiar about the person. Was it simply someone from the store that she knew?

Chase climbed in the truck and handed her the keys. "Ready to roll? Time for some action."

She laughed at his enthusiasm and thought about a different kind of action she could engage him in. That idea made her shiver and forget all about the person in the alley.

CHAPTER 14

$\mathcal{C}$hase was sweating like a pig, sometimes ranch work was damn hard work, and it didn't help they were having a heat wave. They were bailing hay today so not only was it hotter than hell and fricken hard work, it was a filthy job on top of it. He couldn't decide if he wanted to jump in the river or go straight home to a shower when they finished for the day.

His brother was in a horrible mood and refused to talk about it. Chase assumed it had something to do with Cade's date with Tanya. He figured Cade would talk to him about it when he'd sorted it all out and had made a decision. Cade didn't talk through his thoughts but instead weighed everything in his mind, and once he'd come up with a plan he would talk about it. More as verification of the idea than anything else.

The only redeeming factor of the day so far was thinking back to his evening with Katie last night. The movie had been great, and they'd chatted about it while driving home until Katie finally said, "I need to lay down for a minute". Then she'd curled up on the bench seat of his truck and used

82

his leg as a pillow. How she could lay down like that and keep the seat belt on, he had no idea. Plus, he didn't think the split bench seat would be very comfortable.

She'd passed out in seconds however, so he thought the tequila had finally caught up with her. Fortunately, it was late enough there was no traffic. He'd carried her up the stairs to her bed and she hadn't even protested. After pulling her shoes off, he'd dragged a light throw blanket up over her. Then he'd left her keys by the bed and let himself out.

He grinned, wondering how long she'd slept in her clothes. A text from her this morning confirmed she was doing good, even if she was a bit chagrined from falling asleep on him the night before. He'd just sent her a smirking emoji back.

Chase was damn glad when they finally called it a day. Although that's when his brother picked to talk. All Chase could think of was getting the damn hay off of him, it was everywhere, but he sat on one of the bails, so Cade could talk. They had two bailers, so the hay they rolled into the large round bails, but they bailed the straw into the smaller square bails. That made it easier for storage and quick identification.

Chase sat patiently while Cade paced in front of him. "So, I know you've wondered why I stay with Tanya, even though she is a royal pain in the ass."

Chase nodded.

"I never wanted to talk about this, but I just can't deal with her any longer and I'm tired of paying for a mistake I made years ago."

This piqued Chase's interest, but he kept silent knowing his brother would continue on.

"The fact of the matter is the woman is driving me batshit crazy and I can't do it anymore." Cade slumped down onto the haybale and hung his head. "She had an abortion when we were in high school. She didn't tell me about it before she did it and she's kept me dancing on the string in order to keep it a secret."

Chase couldn't help himself when he burst into laughter. He didn't know his brother was quite so gullible. But this bit of news explained so much of why he had put up with that raging bitch for so many years.

Cade looked at him with a scowl. "Just what is so fucking funny about that?"

"Cade, she told every guy in high school that same song and dance. Apparently, you are the only one who actually believed her."

"What?"

"She told everyone that story, every one of the guys she'd slept with for months. Including the boyfriend of one of her inner circle, she'd passed the guy on to her friend with her blessing. So, when Tanya came back to the boy with that story, it pissed the girl off, so she ratted her out. Tanya did not have an abortion. She wasn't even pregnant. Apparently, she did have to have a D&C because of some abnormal bleeding. The guy wasn't supposed to tell anyone of course, but when she told me the same damn thing we talked about it."

"Are you serious, right now? You had sex with Tanya in high school?"

"Cade, everyone did. For me it was only one time, because I realized you liked her. But that was enough for her to tell me that ridiculous story about an abortion. I can count another half dozen guys she told the same thing to."

"Why didn't I know this?"

Chase rubbed a thumb over his mouth as he thought back to that time. "Now that I think about it, the subject came up in a science class, because one of the guys was freaking out. So, we talked about it and several of the other guys were relieved to hear the truth. You weren't in my science class, because you were busy being a math geek."

"So, because I chose to take math instead of science in my senior year, that woman has been torturing me for almost ten years? Well, fuck."

"She wouldn't have if you'd said something earlier."

Cade shook his head. "I was too ashamed, and I felt guilty."

"Now that you know the truth you can move on. Not that you have to break up with her, but she doesn't have anything to hold over your head, either."

Cade looked up with a grin. "She doesn't, does she. So next time she has a hissy fit I can walk away, with no fear or shame."

"Yep."

"Hot damn. That's some good news there. Kristine and Daniel." Cade pointed at him.

"Yep."

"I always wondered why Tanya and Kristine went from besties to not speaking."

"Now you know." Chase scratched at his chest.

Cade nodded. "I'm hot and itchy, do you want to go jump in the river and cool off?"

"Sounds like an excellent idea."

KATIE HAD ONLY a slight headache from her margarita drinking last night. She was grateful to Chase for putting a glass of water, some crackers and a bottle of pain killers next to her bed when he'd taken her home. She'd woken up about two in the morning and had finally gotten into bed after putting on some pajamas and taking the pills.

Overall, she'd had a good time with him last night. Just

the two of them had seemed more like a date. She knew it wasn't, but her foolish heart wouldn't listen to her more sensible head. Dinner had been tasty, and she was looking forward to eating the other half of her burrito for lunch. The movie had been fun, an action film with some humor thrown in and a side of romance. She felt a little bad about falling asleep on the way home. But he'd encouraged her to have the second margarita so part of it was his fault. She'd sent him a sorry text this morning to which he'd responded with a smirk.

She spent the morning stocking the candy aisle, it was looking a little ragged. She didn't have much of a sweet tooth, so it wasn't a challenge for her. She'd hired a kid last summer who spent his whole paycheck on candy. Not all at once, but he'd take one item a day and ask her to take it off his paycheck, at the end of two weeks his take home pay ended up being about ten dollars, even with the employee discount she'd made up for him, because she just couldn't bring herself to give him nothing at all. It had been a hard lesson, but he had learned quickly and reigned his sweet tooth in. He still spent some money on candy, but it was a carefully thought out purchase.

She shook her head at the memory as she heated up her burrito. She would eat it at the front counter, so she could keep an eye on the store, like she did pretty much every day. Normally it was a sandwich and some carrots so today was a real treat.

She set it down and got herself a bottle of water, unscrewing the lid she took a drink and heard the door chime. She turned to greet her customer and noticed it was the girl from a couple of days ago and she was even dirtier and skinnier than she had been. As the girl moved toward the snacks something about her movement tugged at her memory. She didn't know what it was, she shut her eyes and tried to remember.

It hit her hard. The person in the alley last night. She was ninety percent certain it had been this girl. So, if the girl was rooting around in dumpsters and was filthy, just what was going on. Was she homeless? Abandoned? She didn't know how to get the girl to talk to her, so far, she hadn't said a word. Could she even speak? Or was she simply skittish?

The girl came up to the counter and laid a few peanut butter crackers on the counter. Katie noticed her looking intently at the burrito. Dammit, she had to try.

"Hi, back for some more crackers, I see."

The girl nodded and started putting a bunch of coins on the counter. Some of those were as filthy as the girl herself.

"Hey maybe you can help me out. Do you like Mexican food?" Katie waived her hand toward her burrito.

The girl's eyes went wide, and she shuffled back a step, but nodded.

"Me too, but I can't eat the whole thing. It's so delicious, but I never eat leftovers. I usually forget about them until they end up being science experiments in the fridge."

That got a tiny smile out of the girl.

"Anyway, rather than throwing it away I thought you might like to eat it. Then I won't have to feel guilty about not eating it or stuff myself until I explode."

Another small smile and a lingering look at the burrito was all the response she got.

"So, would you eat it? It's a little on the spicy side so you'll need at least one bottle of water, or better yet, milk. I'll pay for one of each in gratitude of you saving my poor stomach and conscience. Deal?"

The girl nodded again so Katie hustled over to the drink cooler and got a large container of milk and an even bigger one of water. She put the water and milk in a bag along with the crackers. Then closed up the register and put the to-go container on top with a package of plastic utensils and napkin. She scooped the change up and handed it back to the girl.

"You keep that for next time. I can't take money from my food savior." She handed the girl the bag. "Thanks so much, for helping me out. There's a nice picnic table across the street in the park over under the trees."

The girl looked like she was going to cry, but quickly nodded and walked out the door and straight to the park. Katie kept an eye on her and watched as she opened the to-go container and the milk and started eating.

Now that she had no lunch, Katie went and got a package of peanut butter crackers. She wouldn't starve and now neither would that kid. As she munched on the crackers she thought about ways to help the girl. Maybe she could get her to trust her enough to tell her what was going on.

She wasn't going to call the Sheriff or CPS until she had more information. Her assumptions about the girl being homeless might not be true at all. She didn't believe that for a second and she hoped the girl had found somewhere safe to be at night. For the most part their town was a safe place unless tourists got out of hand. Or wild animals wandered in. But they didn't see many animals until winter, which was still weeks away.

CHAPTER 15

*K*atie wanted to dress up for Karaoke tonight. Chase was going to come by and park his truck at the store and walk with her to the bar. Not that she was afraid of something happening a second time, but apparently, he wasn't going to take any chances.

She smiled at herself in the mirror, her hair looked pretty and so did the flirty purple dress she'd pulled on. There had been some turmoil in her mind about the dress, she'd thought about wearing something similar the night she'd been accosted. Was that only a week ago? That night she had gone for comfort rather than dressy. After the men had tried to take advantage of her, she'd been so thankful she'd gone with jeans and boots. They had protected her, whereas a dress wouldn't.

But she was damn sure not going to live her life in fear, so she'd pulled out her sexiest dress and awesome black sandals with the four-inch heels. Her makeup was perfection and she'd chosen sparkly jewelry. She was ready to go and prove to herself and the world, that some jerks wouldn't keep her down.

She also had a big advantage from earlier in the day. Happiness was bubbling in her because she'd fixed the home-less girl up with a bag of 'expired' food and some drinks to go with it. The girl had whispered a quiet thank you before scurrying out the door and disappearing. So, it had been a great day in her opinion and she was excited to be going out to have some fun with her bestie. There was no telling if Cade would be there or not, but she would have just as good a time with Chase if he didn't show. If it was all three of them that would be a kicking time too.

There was a knock on the door, so she called out. "Chase?"

"Yep."

"It's open, come on in." She put her last long sparkly earring on and turned away from the mirror and toward the door.

Chase stood in the door wide-eyed and speechless.

She grinned. "So, I look okay?"

He shook his head. "Okay? No, you look fucking awesome."

"Thank you, kind sir. Ready to go?"

He shook his head again and cleared his throat. "Sure, still don't know if Cade is joining us."

"Well if he doesn't it's his loss."

She heard him mutter something as they walked out the door. It sounded like 'that's for damn sure' but it could have been something else. But he'd made her feel confident and powerful, rather than scared or timid and that was exactly what she needed, to get back on the horse so to speak.

Not only that but she'd decided if Cade didn't show, she was going to see if she could get Chase to see her as a woman rather than a buddy. She'd chickened out the other night, but was determined to put those fears into a locked box and give it her best shot. He'd looked interested when he'd picked her up, so was there was a spark of attraction there? She had a plan and she just hoped he wouldn't laugh at her when she completed it.

CHASE WALKED next to Katie toward the bar where they held the Karaoke event on Friday nights. He knew she was talking to him and he really should be paying attention, but his mind was shot. When he'd walked into her home and seen her standing there in that damn sexy dress and the come fuck me heels, he'd lost all power of thought. He was certain she'd worn both before, but that was before that dumbass Tim Jefferson had shown up, and thrown his whole life into chaos by talking about how sexy Katie was.

It was all he could think about, and then when he'd seen her tonight in that beyond sexy outfit, he'd lost his shit, together and forever. It was like his brain had leaked out of this head and pooled on the floor. But he'd learned a long time ago how to keep her talking, so when she paused in her speech he grunted, and she started talking again.

When they walked into the bar, he noticed several men give her the once over, clearly interested, she didn't even notice. He glared at them, until they turned their eyes back to their own dates or friends. No way in hell was he going to allow some idiot to pick her up tonight. He steered her past the crowd to a table he saw available on the side of the room, not far from the dance floor and Karaoke area. He wondered if he could put up a no trespassing sign, to keep the guys away and dearly wished his brother would come and join them, to sit on her other side. But he didn't really hold out any hope in that area since Cade was out with Tanya. Unless she picked a fight with him, and he supposed there was a fifty-fifty chance of that happening.

They ordered some drinks and looked through the Karaoke menu. Several people had signed up ahead of them. Chase chose The Devil Went Down to Georgia by the Charlie Daniels Band, it was a fun song and he pretty much knew it by heart. Katie got a small smirk on her face when she signed up and didn't tell him her song.

They listened to some truly horrible renditions of songs, that made a person want to cry. A couple of people did a really good job with their song and everyone cheered for them. Chase was called up and Katie watched him perform his favorite. She clapped and cheered like crazy when he finished, while a couple of people called out that he needed to expand his repertoire and learn another song.

He simply grinned and shook his head. "You don't mess with perfection, boys."

Which elicited groans and laughs.

When they finally called Katie up for her song she winked at him and told him to pay attention. He turned his chair toward the stage, so he could see better, and told her he'd be cheering for her. She kissed him on the cheek and strutted up to the stage.

CHAPTER 16

*K*atie marched up on stage, she'd specifically asked to be the last singer in the Karaoke line up because she had every intention of making this event a showstopper. On one hand she was scared to death that Chase would think she'd lost her mind and wouldn't be interested. And the entire town would know what she'd done. She had no misconceptions on that part, tomorrow morning everyone in town would know she'd challenged Chase.

On the other hand, she felt powerful and in control. She knew she looked great and she was—by God—going to do this. She was putting it all out there for good or for bad. No shrinking away, no turning back. She was determined to let that man know that she was not a little girl anymore and she wanted an adult relationship with him. Starting today.

She got up to the stage and took the mic in her hand. The music cued up and the words started to scroll across the reader, but she didn't need them, she knew every word. She looked out into the crowd, who in three and a half minutes would be doing exactly what the words said. She was going to give the entire town something to talk about. Bonnie Raitt's song was exactly how she felt about the man sitting across the room.

It didn't take her long to turn her attention to him. There was no way he was getting out of this evening without knowing how she felt. He would have no choice but to acknowledge it. As she sang he watched her like a hawk, there was no laughing or shrugging it off. He was paying attention and getting the message loud and clear.

From the stage it looked like he might be receptive, so she decided to be brave and go for it all the way.

CHASE COULD NOT BELIEVE what he was seeing and hearing. The woman on stage, his best friend forever, was singing directly to him about giving the town something to talk about by the two of them hooking up. She looked so fricken sexy and the words went straight to his blood, making it race enough to give him a heart attack. She was seducing him from the stage and doing a damn fine job of it. His hands were shaking as desire coursed through his body and his heart pounded.

Did she really mean it? Did she think of him night and day? She didn't even look out into the crowd again but stared straight at him and since he was up against a wall he knew for a fact there was no one behind him. He wanted to turn and look just to be sure, but he couldn't tear his eyes off of her.

She belted out the song and looked so damned beautiful he was frozen. He was so confused and filled with such lust he couldn't think straight. When the song ended, she came over and plopped down in his lap. He didn't know what else to do but hold on as she laid a big fat kiss on him. He did not fight her off.

He vaguely heard catcalls as she kissed his brains out. She tasted like heaven and he pulled her closer as she wrapped her arms around his neck and opened her mouth to his. He dove in for more.

When she pulled back he wanted to carry her off into some dark corner. He couldn't do that, and he had no other thoughts. He couldn't think of a thing to say as she stared into his eyes and they panted. Finally, he managed to growl out, "Let's dance."

He pulled her onto the dance floor. As the music flowed over him he held her close. His thoughts whirled but his body moved in close and enjoyed every bit of her.

He finally whispered into her ear, "I don't know what to say, or think, or do."

She rubbed up against him and his eyes crossed in pleasure. "Part of you knows exactly what to do."

"But we're friends."

She let out a huff and pulled back.

He panicked and yanked her in close. "No, I don't mean it like that. I just don't want to hurt our friendship. You are too important to me to fuck this up."

She laid her head on his shoulder for a moment. Then she looked up at him. "Then let's make a pact not to."

"A pact?" he said stupidly.

"Yes, like we did as kids."

He thought back to the hundreds of pacts they'd made as kids. "Blood or pinky."

"Blood, for sure."

"As much as I would like to take you up on this idea, and that is an overwhelming screaming desire, I think we need to think about it some more."

Her shoulders slumped in defeat. "Fine, write up a

contract, think it to death and when you're ready you can let me know." She sighed. "We both have to work in the morning, let's go."

He knew he'd hurt her feelings, but this was too big of a step to take without some serious consideration. There had to be something he could do to lighten the mood.

He leaned in and whispered, "It will give them something to talk about."

She laughed and grinned up at him. He kissed her soundly on the lips and they walked out of the bar hand in hand.

～

KATIE WAS DISAPPOINTED that Chase hadn't taken her up on her offer. But he hadn't laughed at her or told her it was a silly idea. He'd looked and felt plenty interested. So, it was possible she did just need to give him some time to think it through. She'd been thinking about it for ten years.

It was a huge change and perhaps a pact wasn't as silly an idea as how she'd been thinking of it when she'd suggested it. But she wasn't going to let it drift off into nothing either, she was going to stay in his face, so he couldn't ignore the idea of them as more than friends, lovers even.

As they walked up to her back door she asked, "Want to play cards tomorrow?"

He looked at her with a surprised expression. Good she needed to keep the man guessing. "We could do that. Do you want to come out to the ranch when you close up?"

"Sure, that would be fun, maybe some of your family would like to get in on the game too."

He grinned at her and looked more relaxed. "We're always happy to take your money."

"I tell you, one day I am going to beat you."

"You can try, darlin', you can try."

He walked up the steps with her and she unlocked the door. Before he could turn around to leave she took hold of his shirt and pulled him in. She didn't know who kissed who first, but he seemed to be just as eager as she was.

Mouths met and devoured as they kissed on her doorstep. She ran her hands up and gripped his hair to hold him close. He tasted like heaven, and man, and she loved it. Tongues and teeth clashed as they both fought for more. It was glorious. When they needed to breathe he pulled back and gasped for breath. She grinned and said, "Think fast."

Going inside she locked the door and heard him swear before he walked down the stairs. Yep, she had no intention of letting him forget. Not. For. One. Second.

CHAPTER 17

*C*hase had just buckled his belt when his brother walked into his room. He turned. "You're dressed already, what's the—"

His brother's fist smashed into his face and his head snapped back.

"What the fuck is that for?"

"You moved on Katie."

"I did not." He saw his brother's hand fist again. "No, wait, really I didn't."

"The whole fucking town saw you. Are you really going to lie to me? Because that makes me furious."

He glowered at is brother. "No. Now just hold onto your temper and flying fists and let me tell you what really happened last night. Rather than town gossip."

"Fine, talk."

"Since you already have some info I'll do crib notes on the public portion of the evening."

Cade nodded.

"We went to Karaoke. She sang that *Something to Talk About* song directly to me. When it was over she sat on my lap and kissed my brains out. I couldn't think so we danced while I tried to get my brain to work."

"Go on." Cade made an impatient gesture.

Chase rubbed the back of his neck. "Then I hurt her feelings."

Cade frowned at him, so he continued. "I told her we needed to think about this and not jump into anything."

"That makes sense, why did it hurt her feelings?"

"She'd just declared to the whole town that she and I were going to hook up...."

Cade rubbed his chin. "And you told her no. Yeah, I could see that might hurt her feelings or piss her off. But I heard you were kissing on the dance floor and walked out glued to each other."

"Yeah, I didn't want her to be sad, so I told her we could still give them something to talk about. So, we kissed on the dance floor and made it look like we were going somewhere to continue."

"But now everyone thinks you two are an item." Cade glowered.

"Nothing to be done about that, they all thought that thirty seconds into the song. Anyway, I took her home and left her there alone."

Cade pointed at him. "Bullshit. I didn't get home until after one and your truck was nowhere to be found."

"That's because I was driving half way to Grand Junction, thinking. Hell, I didn't even realize where I was, until I was nearly to Craig."

Cade laughed. "That's a hell of a long way for a thinking drive."

Chase shook his head. "It's a lot to think about." He flopped down on his bed. "I don't want to fuck this up and there doesn't seem to be any way to turn back time. She's too important to me, to both of us, to the family even, to blow it."

"Yes, she is. So… don't."

Chase huffed. "Cade, you know very well I've never had a girlfriend over six months. I suck at relationships."

"But those women were not Katie. She won't let you suck at it. Not that I'm fully in favor of all this."

"Join the fricken crowd. I'm not fully in favor of it either. But Katie seems to be. Can you imagine declaring in front of the whole damn town that you want to… well… do whatever it is she wants to do." The idea of that made him sick to his stomach, the woman was clearly made of stronger stuff than he was, there is no way in hell he would declare himself before the whole town.

"Have sex with you? Be your girlfriend? No, I can't imagine doing anything of that sort in front of the whole town. I can't imagine Katie doing it."

"Believe me I was shocked as hell by it."

They both sat there in silence for a while.

Chase sighed. "She's coming over tonight to play cards."

Cade's head snapped toward him. "After you shut her down?"

"I didn't shut her down, exactly. I told her we needed to think about it. Maybe make a pact on how to handle it."

Cade guffawed. "Blood or pinky?"

Chase shrugged. "Blood, too important for anything else."

Cade shook his head. "You are such a dumbass."

"Believe me, I know. What in the hell is she thinking anyway?"

KATIE WAS PLOTTING. She'd made her move last night and Chase hadn't told her she was an idiot or laughed at her. He'd taken her seriously and wanted to think about it. That was good, right?

Now how was she going to get past the thinking, to the doing? That was the question. She'd felt his interest in his body, which had responded to her song, and kiss in a very gratifying manner. But he clearly was not some kid who was led around by his dick, he hadn't acted on that arousal. Dammit.

She supposed she should be grateful that he didn't want to screw up their friendship by leaping in before they both had time to think about it. But she was frustrated by the whole idea. She didn't want to wait, she'd been waiting ten years already and he was finally looking at her like a woman.

So now she was plotting how to keep him interested. She had to think of ways to tempt him into taking the next step.

The door chimed, and she looked up from her notes to see the homeless girl slink in. The girl scanned the empty store and came over to her.

"Hi, how are you today? I'm so glad you stopped by. I was wondering if you could do me a favor."

The girl just looked at her. So, she continued, "I've been so busy the last couple of days I haven't had time to sweep. I was wondering if I could pay you to help me with that."

The girl looked around the empty store and raised an eyebrow.

"Oh, I know it doesn't look like I'm busy, but it's... um... inventory time and I have to get my books together for that."

The girl looked at the counter and saw the paper she'd been doodling on.

Katie looked down and saw it was filled with hearts and Chase's initials. She flipped it over. "That's some designs I'm working on for some... um... advertising. Anyway, would you be able to help? I'll pay you eight dollars an hour, that's a little under minimum wage but you probably aren't old enough to fall under that law. Plus, I thought I could just pay you cash so it would be kind of as a favor to me rather than a full-fledged employee. Are you interested?"

The girl looked at her like she was trying to decide if she was being honest, which she mostly was. Not the needing help part, but all the rest.

Finally, the girl nodded, and Katie felt relief slide through her. "Oh, and lunch is part of the job too. Come with me."

Katie showed her where the broom and dustpan were and told her to start wherever she wanted. When they stopped for lunch Katie was going to see if she could get the girl to tell her her name, or at least something she could call her.

Katie got the financial ledgers out and brought them up to the counter that way it wouldn't look like she'd lied to the girl. She should have thought through her story a bit more before voicing it. But she was thrilled the girl was going to take her up on the offer. She decided she would come up with something the girl could do every day for a few hours, at least that would give her enough money to eat.

As she fussed with the books, checked out customers, and plotted against Chase, she wracked her brain for projects for the girl to do. When it got to be lunch time Katie called the café to see if they could run her a couple of sandwiches across the street.

When the sandwiches arrived, she asked the pharmacist to watch the store while she and the girl ate some lunch in the break room. Which really was a tiny room with a coffeepot and a microwave and a tiny table with two chairs. But it worked for her purposes.

She grabbed some water and then thought the girl needed milk and brought some of that with her too. She walked up to the girl carefully sweeping up a lot more dirt than Katie thought she would and asked her to come join her for lunch.

The girl nodded and carefully swept the dirt into the dustpan and emptied it, before carrying it all with her to the back. Katie had to wonder if the girl had some retail knowledge, because most kids her age would just drop everything where they were and go to lunch.

Katie washed her hands in the little sink and the girl did the same before sitting down at the tiny table. Katie handed the girl her food and drink. They both started eating and Katie watched and waited to see when the girl relaxed.

When the girl had nearly finished her lunch Katie casually asked. "So, can you tell me your name, or is there something I can call you?"

There was a moment of panic in her eyes, but she fought it back and murmured, "Gwen."

Katie felt like throwing confetti. "Gwen, what a pretty name. Did I ever tell you my name is Katie?"

Gwen nodded.

"You know I noticed what a good worker you are. If you aren't busy tomorrow I could use some help again."

Gwen looked at her and nodded, then she picked up her trash and threw it into the can, and went back to sweeping.

CHAPTER 18

*K*atie was ready for phase two of her campaign to tempt Chase into a romantic relationship. She had on some jeans that fit her to perfection, and a dark blue flirty top with most of the shoulders cut out, and some of the cutest boots ever. Her makeup was understated but brought out her eyes and lips. She wanted him looking at her lips, so he'd think about kissing them again. Her hair was loose but curled in big fat curls, and she'd spritzed on the perfume he'd bought her for Christmas.

She was armed for battle or should she just call it what it was, seduction. Yes, she was going to try to seduce the man and she didn't care if the whole family was there to watch. They'd probably all heard about her antics last night anyway, so it didn't matter much. She hoped like hell he wouldn't be able to resist her.

In her purse, which she tossed into the front seat of her car, was the pact she'd written up. It was fairly simple, basically just saying that if they decided to break up, they would not let it get in the way of their friendship. She wasn't quite sure how that would work but he was right, their friendship was too important to give it up over a failed relationship. On the other hand, she wasn't going to wonder for the rest of her life what might have happened if they hadn't given it a shot.

She pulled her old jalopy onto the road pointed out of town. One of these days she needed to think about getting a new car. She'd had this one since she'd graduated from high school, many years ago.

As she drove, Katie contemplated the fact that she fully intended to tempt Chase into giving them a chance at love. Maybe she could get Cade on board to help her convince Chase. That is provided she could convince Cade this was a good idea. She had no idea how he would react to her plans for his brother. He might think it was great fun and help her, or he might not like it at all.

She didn't think he would be jealous, he was always with some woman, mostly Tanya if she was honest. Although he and Tanya broke up several times a year, and it never took Cade long to find a new girl to date. He was too much fun, every woman she'd ever known had wanted to date him.

The ranch came into view and she turned into the long driveway that led to the ranch, she drove under the sign showing the Rockin' K brand, up the gravel drive, and parked to see Tony playing in the back yard. He whooped and ran toward her as she climbed out of the car.

"Miss Katie, what are you doing here? Are you here to ride horses with my uncles? It's gonna be dark soon, so I don't think that's a good idea." He shook his head to emphasize his point. Then brightened and grinned at her. "Did you bring candy with you?

"I came over to see you and your whole family. You're right it's too late to ride horses so perhaps we will play cards instead. Of course, I brought candy."

"Yay for candy. I play slap jack with my uncles sometimes. Are you going to play slap jack too?"

"Probably not tonight. Do you want to help me carry in the candy?"

He jumped up and down. "Yes, yes, yes."

She laughed and handed him a small bag she had ready for him to carry. Just then Chase walked out of the barn and her heart skipped a beat. Dear God, the man was sexy, she had to work to keep from melting into a puddle of lust. He'd clearly been working out in the fields. His shirt was hanging from his back pocket and he was covered in sweat, dust and hay pieces. She wanted to help him wash that dirt off that fine chest and back.

He grinned at her like he knew what she was thinking, and took the larger bags of candy out of her hands. His eyes roamed her body and then came back up to settle on her lips before finally reaching her eyes. "Howdy, Katie. You're looking mighty pretty tonight." He sniffed. "And you smell good too. Is that the perfume I bought you for Christmas?"

She couldn't speak. The man had just sniffed her. She nodded stupidly.

He gave her a hot look. "Let's get this candy in, so I can go take a shower and wash this dirt off. You can distribute your candy while I do that, and then I'll be happy to take your money."

She followed him into the house, into the kitchen without saying a word. When she could finally think again she pointed at him. "I plan to take yours tonight, Chase."

He barked out a laugh. "Right. Keep dreaming, sweetheart."

Katie watched him walk away and kept staring at where he had disappeared until someone cleared their throat and reminded her she had an audience. She turned and saw expectant expressions on each family member and ranch hand.

So, before anyone could say anything she cleared her throat. "So, I imagine most of you have heard about me singing Karaoke last night. Yes, it was all me. I picked the song and I sang it to Chase, fully intending to seduce him. I decided that it was time to let my feelings be known, so I picked a very public venue to do it in, that way it can't be ignored or swept under the rug. In light of that I will tell you all that I plan to push Chase into giving a relationship with me a chance, other than that of just best friends. I hope you won't mind or feel odd about it. In fact, I hope you support me. I've wanted to do this for ten years. I'm asking you to approve."

They all nodded slowly. Grandpa K spoke up, "You and Chase are adults and can do as you wish. You're like family, Katie, and always welcome." He looked around at the rest of the family and crew gathered around. "But what we're really doing here is waiting for our candy."

Yeah, now if the floor would just open up and swallow her that would be great. Her cheeks bloomed with color and she started handing out the candy as quickly as possible. If she gave the wrong bag to the wrong person they would have to figure it out, because she wanted to go hide.

CHASE WENT UP TO SHOWER. If they'd been alone and not surrounded by his family, he was pretty certain she would have joined him in the shower. She'd looked at him like he was a popsicle on a hot day and she wanted to lick him from stem to stern. He knew he was filthy and smelled like sweat and dirt and hay, so why she looked at him like that was a miracle in itself.

He wasn't going to argue though he'd have been more than happy to share a shower with her she'd looked so pretty standing there. He was flattered she'd worn the perfume he'd given her, the perfume simply enhanced her normal smell and made him want to carry her off to the nearest flat surface.

But she was downstairs with his entire family handing out candy and… shit were they giving her the third degree? They all probably had heard the same rumors that Cade had by now. He shouldn't have left her alone with them until they had made some decisions.

Chase hurried through his shower imagining the worst. He dragged on jeans and a plaid shirt, tucking it in even as he hurried down the hall. He hoped no one was giving her a hard time. He breathed a sigh of relief when he found her alone at the kitchen table.

He rushed in, over to her. "Was it horrible? Did they ask a ton of questions? I'm sorry I should have stayed with you until the barrage was over. Can you forgive me for leaving you?"

She looked at him with a dazed expression. "Yes, it was horrible. They were all just standing there looking at me, so I told them what I had done, and why, and asked them to support our relationship. Grandpa K virtually patted me on the head, and said they didn't really care what we did, since we were adults, and that I was always welcome. But could they have their candy now?"

Chase barked out a laugh and sat at the table. "That's it? Really? Well, you got off easier than I did then. Cade punched me right in the face for making a move on you."

She gasped and snapped her head toward him, her eyes searching his face. "Oh, you poor thing. I do see a bit of a bruise on your jaw. I'm kind of surprised it isn't worse looking."

"Yeah, he pulled the punch, otherwise he would have knocked me to the floor. I didn't see it coming. Didn't expect it at all."

"Here let me kiss it and make it all better." She climbed into his lap and kissed the bruising she could just barely see under his beard.

Emma came in the kitchen. "Just because we all approve of you working on a different kind of relationship, doesn't mean we want to see it. Now, stop that."

Chase held Katie from jumping off his lap and grinned at his sister. "Jealous, Em?"

She sighed. "Yes, I suppose I am."

Katie elbowed him and got off his lap, darn it. He was enjoying her all snuggled up to him. "But we don't have to flaunt it either. Now let's just play cards. Does anyone else want to play?"

Chase said, "I did tell everyone, but they all had plans. Cade's out with Tanya, Emma has books to work on, the engaged and married sibs begged off to entertain themselves. Mom, Dad and Grandpa K are busy too. Oh, and Drew's on shift tonight. So, it's just the two of us."

She sighed. "Well, I suppose I can take your money."

He guffawed. "Riiiight."

"Don't be an ass, it could happen. Get the stuff."

He grinned at her, not the least bit worried about her playing better, she had to be the worst card player on the planet. Besides the fact, they played for pennies. The poker chips and the cards were in a convenient wooden carousel that was probably older than he was. His parents and grandparents had loved to play.

He could remember when his parents would invite over another two couples and they would play late into the night. The kids from all three families would play together until it got too late, and then the adults would take a break and get them all into pajamas', and they would all lay down in the big beds together to tell stories and giggle, until they fell asleep. When the playing was done the other families would be bundled out to the cars for the drive home and their parents would help them get to their own beds. Sometimes they went to the other family's homes, which provided them with another adventure, but it was often at theirs. Maybe because they had the largest household.

Chase got the poker chips set out of the cupboard, while Katie got them drinks.

There was a can of mixed nuts he'd picked up for her. She was a salty snack kind of person, and she'd brought him a bag of chocolate covered raisins.

They sat and he dealt the cards calling out the game and the wild cards. He hoped that when people finished up what they were doing they would come join them. Poker was more fun with four to six people playing.

His mind skittered down a path where it would be more fun to play poker just the two of them. Strip poker would be fun, except she would end up completely naked while he was fully dressed. Not that he would mind that. He wondered if he could talk her into it if they bumped their relationship up. He played loosely with his mind engaged in his fantasies.

When he laid his cards down, she crowed. "I won. Yay! I told you I could do it."

He looked at his cards and hers and sure enough she had won. Since he hadn't really been paying attention he wasn't completely sure he hadn't screwed it up.

"Yeah, well, that was a once in a lifetime phenomenon." He would pay attention this time.

She shuffled the cards and dealt out the first round of seven card stud. He grinned internally and figured without wild cards he'd beat her for sure. He was surprised as hell when she took that round too. He had shit in his hand and she'd ended up with two pair, threes and sevens.

He racked up the cards and dealt again while she smugly ate some nuts. He dealt the next hand and watched her face go more radiant with each card he laid down. He knew he should fold, she obviously had a great hand, and had no poker face whatsoever. But on the table he was winning, she had a single ace and he had a pair of fours, he wanted to push her, so he bet high. High for them, which was a whopping ten cents. She happily pushed her chips into the center and then raised him another five, before he dealt the final card. She nearly whooped in excitement.

Alyssa had just walked into the kitchen and had seen Katie's face. "Katie you're not supposed to show you are happy with your cards. Let me see what you have." Katie showed Alyssa her hidden cards and a huge grin lit Alyssa's face. "Alrighty then, I see why you can't contain it. Carry on."

Chase groaned internally and saw Alyssa leave the kitchen without whatever she'd come in for.

"There is no way you can beat me this time, Chase. That's three hands in a row. I'm on a roll."

He called, hoping she was trying to get him to fold, but no. She grinned as she flipped over an eight of clubs, which matched the eight of diamonds on the table. He raised his eyebrows at that paltry start and then she flipped over two more aces, not wild cards, she had three natural aces. The Ace of Diamonds, the Ace of Spades and the Ace of Hearts. He just stared at the cards like they had betrayed him and then turned over his third four which was a wild card. And this time she did whoop as she raked in her pot of a whopping eighty-two cents.

"I told you I could win." She wiggled in her chair while she gathered the cards to deal. She had a huge grin on her face.

Alyssa and Beau came in as she dealt. "Do you want to play?" she asked.

Beau shook his head. "Nope, just came to watch you clean his clock. My dear brother could use some humility."

Alyssa nodded. "Yeah he's been a little too cocky about always beating you."

The woman won the next two hands as Beau and Alyssa cheered her on. Chase couldn't believe he had to dig more money out of his wallet to buy chips.

He finally won the next hand, but it was a small one and he just barely won it. He started to wonder if his luck had changed or if the Poker gods were smiling on her, or what. He saw Beau text something on his phone and a few minutes later when his brother Adam and his fiancé, Rachel, walked in.

Adam said, "We didn't come to play. We just heard the 'stud' of seven card stud was losing his britches to the little lady of bad luck."

Rachel snapped a picture of Katie with her large pile of chips and glorious smile. Chase's mind went blank from that luminous smile and he couldn't remember his name, let alone how to play cards. So, he lost another two hands.

His sister Emma came in next. "I had to get Tony down and finish up the accounting before I could join in cheering Katie on. I see you're still kicking butt and taking names."

Katie's smile could light up the next three counties with no problem at all.

She said, "I do seem to be doing better tonight."

Emma nodded. "It seems to me this turning over a new leaf and going for what you want has had a positive effect on you."

Cade came whooshing in the door. "I got rid of Tanya and came as quick as I could. I'll probably catch holy hell tomorrow, but I couldn't miss this."

Chase glared at his twin. "Just whose side are you on anyway?"

"Katie's." They all said in unison.

"Traitors." He grumped but was enjoying the excitement he saw reflected in Katie's face, and had to admit he was on her side, too.

CHAPTER 19

K atie was on cloud nine, she'd had so much fun playing cards last night. The fact that she'd won eleven dollars and eighty-four cents was exciting, but the real pleasure had been Chase's whole family cheering her on. It made her feel welcome and after her declaration of how she felt about Chase, it seemed to her like it was also meant as a stamp of approval, about their moving to the next level.

They'd all had such a good time and although Chase had pretended to be grumpy about losing, she knew he wasn't really, and was enjoying it as much as anyone else.

He'd walked her to the car after he ran out of cash. When they got to the car he looked around.

She asked him. "What are you looking for?"

"Dolly."

"Why are you looking for Dolly?"

"So, she can bump into you and send you falling into my arms, like she did a few weeks ago. I think she was match-making and I was too stupid to see it."

She laughed. "I'll bet she was, but you don't need Dolly. I am happy to fall into your arms any time they are open."

With a grin he opened his arms and she walked into them. He kissed her stupid and then said something about a poker rematch. A rematch with no money. When she looked at him confused, he explained how to play strip poker in a very detailed way that ended up with her squirming and wet.

Then he kissed her again before he bundled her into her car.

She rolled down her window and asked, "Just how am I supposed to be able to drive in this state?"

Leaning down into the car his breath caressed her face as he whispered, "Very slowly and carefully. I don't want to miss out on that rematch."

Her breath backed up in her throat and she nodded before starting the car. Once she was free of the danger zone, a smile had lit her face that stayed there all the way home.

When she finally got in her door she decided to tease him a bit herself. So, she stripped out of her clothes and laid them carefully arranged on the chair in her room with the underwear on top. Then she took a picture and texted it to him saying she'd arrived home safe and sound, and it was too bad he wasn't there to enjoy her clothes being on the chair, instead of on her body.

He texted her back and told her she was a naughty woman for putting those thoughts in his head. She laughed and sent him back a kissy face emoji and 'sweet dreams'. Then she pulled on her pajamas and had fallen asleep to dreams of playing strip poker with the man. It appeared he was planning to take her up on her offer of more. Now they just had to decide when and where.

Katie thought about when they could proceed as she stocked the dairy cooler, she pulled out each item, checked the date to make sure it had not expired while she rotated in the new products. There were a couple of items that needed to be used today or tomorrow at the latest. Rather than throwing them away she saved them for Gwen, the girl could probably use the calcium. She found one that she must have missed last time that was a few days expired, that one went into the trash. Even though it was only a couple of days past the sell date. She didn't want to take any chances.

She usually was able to get all the coolers done in one morning, as long as she didn't have too many customers. Sometimes in the summer—when she was slammed—it took her a whole week to cycle through all the cold food and drinks All those tourists were good for sales, but it was a lot of work keeping up with them, maintaining the products, and keeping the place clean. She really could use a year-round helper, not just the summer candy addict. Gwen had already assisted in a lot of ways; the girl was a good worker. It's too bad she was so young. *I really need to try to get her to open up, she clearly needs help.*

Katie pondered how to do that in between thoughts of her and Chase. They hadn't talked about a pact again, she hadn't shown him what she'd written up. They probably should at least have a discussion about how they planned to remain friends if anything went south. Lots of things to think about as she went about the mundane work of running the store.

When Gwen came into the store later that morning Katie had thought up a plan to see if she could get her to open up, at least a little. She was very worried about the girl and wanted to help get her in whatever way she could. But first she needed to know what that was.

"Hi Gwen. Good to see you." Good grief the girl was getting dirtier every day. But at least she didn't look so hungry. "I thought you could keep working on the shelves. The ones you have finished are so clean and sparkly."

Gwen smiled and nodded.

"When you get finished, I have a huge favor to ask you. One of the bath salts people sent me some samples and asked for feedback on them. One of the samples is for a fragrance that always makes me sneeze, so I was wondering if you could try them out for me."

Gwen started to shake her head no, so Katie barreled on, "And if you wouldn't mind terribly I would like you to try them out up in my apartment before you leave for the day. He wants to know today if possible and I haven't been able to find anyone else to help. There is also a shampoo sample if you wouldn't mind. I know it's kind of an awkward thing to do for someone, but I would really appreciate it."

Gwen finally said quietly, "I wouldn't mind."

"Great, that's just great. Thanks so much I really appreciate it." Once Gwen was settled on that idea, Katie was going to mention that she'd cleaned out her closet the other day and had some clothes she needed to take to charity, but since they were becoming friends she wanted Gwen to have first pick of anything she wanted.

At the end of the four hours that Gwen worked for her, Katie had the Pharmacist watch the store while she took Gwen upstairs. She showed her the clothes and Gwen was happy to take two shirts, two pairs of jeans and some underwear. Katie made up some BS about needing to run a load of laundry and volunteered to wash Gwen's clothes in with hers to make a full load.

When Gwen came out of the bathroom a few minutes later she looked like a new person. Her smile was radiant, and she was so clean. Katie put her new clothes into a grocery bag and told Gwen she would have her other clothes ready for her tomorrow. She'd given Gwen a small kit of travel items that had a mini hairbrush and some other things she thought the girl could use.

117

Katie had made up some bogus questions to ask Gwen about the sample. Each one would sound like it was about the product but would subtly find out more about the girl. Like if she was from around here and recognized the scent. Sneaky questions.

She and Gwen went back down into the store, so Katie could give her the milk and her pay. Just as they were finished with that Chase walked in the door. Katie grinned at him, but she noticed that Gwen moved back away from him, like he was a scary guy and her expression had turned fierce.

Chase walked right past the girl. He looked so damn hot in his good jeans and western shirt. "I came over to see if you wanted to hang out tonight, here at your place where we have more privacy."

He waggled his eyebrows at her and made her blush. "We could do that. Want to get us a pizza or something for dinner?"

"You read my mind. I'll be back in a while."

When Chase left, Katie noticed that Gwen was gone, too.

CHASE WHISTLED as he walked down the street to the pizza place. He hoped to take Katie up on the offer she'd given him the other night, but he supposed they needed to talk first. He couldn't do that out in public or at his house, so he'd decided to drive into town and see if she was amenable to spending the night in.

He'd been gratified at her delight in seeing him and also in the blush that told her she'd been thinking about the two of them together also. He figured it was time to move forward or try to go back to 'just friends'. He had a pocket full of condoms, just in case. He laughed at himself knowing

118

it would be a short trip to get more if they needed them, since she stocked them in her store.

He ordered a large pizza, half her favorite, which was Canadian bacon and pineapple, and half his favorite, which was pepperoni and black olives. He got them a salad to go with it, and some breadsticks because they both loved them dipped in marinara sauce. It was nice to know exactly what to order since he already knew what she loved.

It was kind of an odd sensation dating someone he knew so well, but in some ways, it was very freeing. There were no games to be played. Or wondering if he was getting the wrong food or if she was going to be glad to see him. He liked this. Now if they could just manage to work the rest out.

He grabbed a bottle of her favorite wine from the liquor store while he waited for the pizza. And since it was right there, a little flowering plant from the florist on the corner. He grinned knowing she would love both of them.

When he got back to the store her evening clerk had arrived, so she told him goodnight and they went up to her apartment.

"I bought you a plant."

"I see that. Why did you?"

He grinned at the clever idea he'd thought up to explain buying it. "I thought it could be our pact's witness."

She snickered. "Our pact's witness?"

"Yeah like we make our pact and every time we see the plant it reminds us of it."

"Oh, I get it." She got plates out and set them on the table. "So, what does our pact look like?"

"Well, the way I see it, is we promise to stay friends no matter what." He opened the wine which was a chilled white wine, so no breathing required. "If one of us wants out of the relationship the other promises to understand. That we keep

119

the other person's best interest in mind at all times, but that doesn't mean you are trapped forever with me if you want out."

She opened the salad and divided it between the two of them and opened the marinara cup and set it between them with the breadsticks. "I guess that sounds reasonable. Not very romantic, but reasonable."

"You want romantic? I can do romantic." He handed her the glass of wine he'd poured and then brought her other hand up to kiss her knuckles.

She laughed. "Riiiight."

"I can try, but the point of the pact is a call for unity between us, before we move our relationship from friend to lover." He dunked a breadstick into the marinara and took a big bite whiles she speared her salad.

"I suppose that's true, having us unified in thoughts and expectations will go a long way toward maintaining our friendship regardless of where this road takes us."

He waved his fork at her before he stabbed at his salad. "My thoughts exactly."

They continued to talk through their ideas on the relationship change as they ate salad and breadsticks. When they finished those and moved on to pizza they realized they were also finished with that topic and started chatting about the upcoming rodeo and town celebration.

He'd chosen not to enter the rodeo competition this year, whining about getting older and not wanting to go up against a cranky bull. Last year he'd been up against an enraged giant and he'd gotten a little torn up.

"It's a young man's sport."

She laughed. "And you're all of twenty-seven. One foot in the grave for you, old man."

He flicked her on the arm. "I saw you all pale-faced and

worried about me. In fact, didn't you tell me I was getting too old and needed to stay off those mean critters?"

She looked away. "Maybe, but I can still reserve the right to tease you."

"Fine by me."

CHAPTER 20

atie was a little nervous about the next portion of the evening. They'd been very sensible and talked through their expectations. But now that they were winding down on dinner her thoughts had turned to sex. Moving from the kitchen to the bedroom was a strange transition. She didn't know what to do next.

She jumped up from the table and started clearing it, putting the left-over wine and food away. Chase loaded the dishwasher and then stopped her as she went back to the table.

He pulled her into his arms and held her.

She was practically quivering.

He rocked her in his arms. "Shhh it's all right, it's just you and me. We don't have to do anything in particular tonight unless we want to."

She relaxed in his warm embrace. "I want to, Chase. I just don't know how to make the transition. Singing for you in my flirty dress to a sexy song was easy. Sitting eating pizza is not exactly enticing."

He tipped her chin up and kissed her slowly, reverently.

Then little by little he ramped up the heat, one tiny bit at a time. He had her panting by the time he pulled back and started feathering kisses over her face. Her eyes, her nose and her cheeks. He nibbled and nipped at her earlobe and she shivered, so he did it again before kissing her neck down to her shoulder. He licked a path of fire at the base of her neck, over to the other shoulder, and repeated his actions in reverse, until he ended back up at her mouth.

She grabbed him by the hair and attacked that warm mouth with a passion of her own. When they came up for air she realized he'd nudged her all the way into her room. She hadn't even noticed.

"That was sneaky of you."

"Not sneaky, just taking the anxiety out." He fastened his mouth back on hers and ran his hands over her body. She purred in the back of her throat, it was delicious in every way.

Katie reached for his shirt and yanked it open, a woman had to love cowboy fashion. Snaps were so much quicker than buttons. She put her hands on all that warm flesh. His muscles bunched as she caressed each one. When she ran her fingers over his nipples and pinched them she felt his cock leap in response. Untucking the shirt from his jeans helped her to reach his back where she gave each muscle the same attention as the front.

He shrugged out of his shirt. "You have entirely too many clothes on, pretty girl."

She looked down. "You might have a point." She yanked her work polo shirt over her head and tossed it on the floor, giving him a view of her lacy bra. "Better?"

He hummed and cupped both breasts, running his thumbs over her nipples. "Much."

Lightening shot from her nipples throughout her whole body, pooling in her stomach. He reached behind her and unhooked her bra, pulling the straps down her arms until she was free. Chase took a good long look.

"So beautiful." He caressed her breasts and then bent down to pull one turgid peak into his mouth, as fireworks shot through her body. She gripped his hair to keep him right where he was.

He chuckled, and the vibration caused more sensations to rise. He switched to the other side and gave it the same attention, while she held on for dear life.

"Chase."

He hummed sending more vibrations through her. "Right here, darling."

She yanked on his hair pulling his head up to fasten her lips on his clever mouth and pressing her chest up against his. The feeling was exquisite. He hugged her close, so she assumed it was good for him as well.

She ran her hands down his back to grip his ass and pull him in closer.

He groaned as she rubbed against him. "Still too many clothes."

"I couldn't agree more, let's lose them. Race you."

He laughed as he pulled back to fumble at his fly.

She yanked her zipper down and pushed both the jeans and her panties to the floor in one quick move, kicked them to the side then pulled her socks off, having left her shoes at the door when they came in.

Chase grumped. "Not fair. I have a button fly which is already strained and cowboy boots on."

He looked up. "Although I'm not complaining given the delightful vision before me."

He reached for her and she pushed his hands away. "Not until you're naked too. It's not fun for just one of us to be unclothed."

He gave her a sly look. "Oh, I could make it fun for you."

All sorts of naughty ideas flashed in her brain and caused more heat to pool in her belly. She blushed. "I suppose you could." She waved her hand at him to keep him moving.

He grinned and finally got the rest of his fly unbuttoned. He yanked off his cowboy boots and socks then pushed his jeans and shorts down, stepping out of them. When he stood back up his erection stood out from his body and he had a handful of condoms.

She grinned and took one of the condoms and ripped it open. As she rolled it on his cock she spoke to it. "Well hello, are you ready for some fun?"

CHASE BARKED out a laugh at her, while at the same time got harder and more aroused. He didn't think that it was possible to laugh with so much fire shooting through his veins, but she managed to cause both of them to happen at the same time.

He wondered how much that had to do with their friendship and being so relaxed with each other, and how much of it was just Katie's fun-loving personality. She squeezed him, and he couldn't think any longer at all. He had no choice but to follow her as she drew him back with her toward the bed. He now had firsthand knowledge and the experience of being led around by his dick, and he found he didn't mind it one little bit.

She let go of him to shove the extra pillows on the floor and tug the comforter and blankets down to the foot of the bed. He got an excellent view of her very fine ass as she did that. The woman was built like a goddess, she was a pocket Venus with her small stature and lovely curves.

She climbed on the bed and patted the mattress in invitation. He didn't have to be asked twice. But he didn't move next to her, instead he started at the end of the bed at her toes and kissed and nibbled his way up her body. She squirmed and tried to cajole him into hurrying. But this was his first time with her and he was determined to wring every bit of pleasure out of the experience.

When he got to her pleasure center he didn't stop and linger, but continued his way up her body until he reached her lips, where he gave her a long lingering kiss.

She panted. "Stop teasing. I want you inside now."

He shook his head. "But I have so many more areas to explore." He started to move back down her body.

She grabbed his hair and yanked. "Oh no you don't. I want you inside now. You can explore later."

She held him firmly and looked so fierce he relented. He didn't plan to leave tonight, so she was right, there was plenty of time for more exploration.

He sighed dramatically. "If you insist." Crawling over on top of her he nestled between her legs. She took him in hand and guided him into her body. She was hot, and wet, and tight. He pushed into her and her body took him in and made room for him. When he was fully seated within her, she tilted her hips, wrapped her legs around his waist and he slid in deeper. He groaned in pleasure, then started loving her with long smooth strokes.

She met him stroke for stroke as they climbed the hill of passion and pleasure together. Slowly it built until they could contain the sensations no longer, and they crested the hill and flew. His body spent, he pressed her into the mattress. When he regained his strength, he tried to roll off of her, but she held him tight with arms and legs.

"Not yet," she said breathlessly.

"But you need to breathe."

"I will in a minute, but I like you where you are."

He pushed up onto his elbows, so he could stay there and let her breathe at the same time. "How's that?"

She smiled up at him, a sexy siren of a smile. "Perfect."

He felt his cock twitch in appreciation. She squeezed him with her inner muscles and his cock twitched again. "Now you stop that, bad girl. I need a few seconds before I'll be ready for round two."

She squeezed him again. "I'm not sure all of you agrees with that assessment."

He put his forehead to hers. "You're trying to kill me, aren't you?"

"Nope just getting my money's worth."

He laughed. "What money is that?"

She slapped him on the ass. "It's an expression, Chase. You don't have to take everything so literal."

"This wasn't supposed to happen."

"What wasn't supposed to happen?"

"Having fun and joking around while laying here, still inside you."

She leaned up and kissed his nose. "Of course, it is. We are still the same people we've always been, so there will have to be laughing and silliness, naked or not."

"I suppose you are right and I was wrong."

"I'm glad you've discovered that early in this relationship. It speaks well of the future," she said primly.

He laughed and rolled them over, so she was on top, where he could tickle her.

She squirmed. "Stop, Chase, no tickling during sex."

He felt his body start to respond to her squirming. "Hey, you're the one who said we had to have fun and laughing. Besides now all your wiggling has encouraged my body to get ready for round two."

"Oh goody, let's switch out the condoms so we can get after it."

He chuckled and sat up. "Have you always been so insatiable about sex?"

She shook her head sadly. "Nope, it's all your fault."

He grinned as he tossed the used condom in the trash and retrieved a new one. "Can't get enough of me?"

"Don't get cocky. Last time you did that I won twelve dollars off of you."

He rolled the new condom on and groaned. "Don't remind me."

She patted his chest. "It was good for you."

Growling he lunged at her. "I'll show you good for me." He snagged both of her wrists pulling them above her head and encircled them both with one hand, while the other explored her curves and hidden treasures. He kissed her neck, and ears, and throat, while she quivered at his touch. The scent of her arousal filling the room.

When she started to beg him to stop, he covered her mouth with his, and let his hand bring her to climax, twice.

CHAPTER 21

*I*n the morning Katie woke slowly with Chase spooning her from behind. One hand was wrapped around her breast. The man had worn her out last night. She'd never believed in multiple orgasms, until he'd firmly proven her wrong. He'd used nearly every portion of his anatomy to bring her to climax after climax. She was so relaxed she wasn't sure she had enough strength left in her body to even be able to climb out of bed. She had some aches and tenderness from all the sexual gymnastics, but it was the best kind of soreness and she hoped to repeat it often.

But it was time for her to get ready for work. She didn't want to leave the warm bed and the warm man, but duty called. She tried to ease away from him, but he tightened his hold and kissed her shoulder.

His voice was gruff with sleep when he asked, "Just where do you think you're going, little miss?"

"To the shower and then to work."

He looked over her shoulder at the clock. "It's early, you don't open for an hour and I pawned off my early chores on my brothers, so I could come in later. Stay here and let's fool around some more."

"As much as I would like to, I don't have time. I have to shower, get dressed, eat breakfast and be down there to open…" she looked at the clock, "…in fifty-eight minutes."

"Tell you what, I'll grab us both breakfast from the café, then we can fool around now, or in the shower, maybe both, and you'll still be to work on time."

"You drive a hard bargain, but I don't think we'll have time for both, so you can meet me in the shower." She pulled quickly away and scampered into the bathroom.

They wasted a lot of water and just barely got clean, but it was the very best shower in the history of showers, in her opinion anyway.

She was grinning as she unlocked the door and he walked across the street to get them breakfast. It was so natural the two of them being together. There had been no awkwardness like normally happened the morning after sex. It had been free and easy, just like sleepovers they'd had in the past only this one included shower sex.

She was having the time of her life and she suspected he was enjoying it too. It was early in this new phase of their relationship, but she couldn't see any reason that would stop them from a more permanent one. Better to not count her chickens before they hatched, however. She would just enjoy where they were going and not think about the future.

They stood behind the counter to eat, so they weren't in the way if customers came in, he'd brought tea for her and coffee for himself. She liked one scrambled egg with a tiny bit of cheddar cheese on top and he got a three-egg omelet with as much meat as they could pack into it, ham, bacon, sausage. He completed his breakfast with hash brown potatoes and wheat toast and then split a cinnamon roll with her. She loved cinnamon rolls but never indulged in them unless he was with her and would eat most of it. So, it was always a treat when they had breakfast together.

Three women came in just as they were finishing up, so she gave him a small peck and sent him on his way. Before the women were fully checked out, he came back in, and he looked fit to be tied. She hurriedly finished ringing up the women, so she could find out what the problem was. As the door shut behind the women she rushed over to him where he was talking on his cell.

"Yeah at Katie's. I'll wait. No. I didn't touch anything. I know the drill."

He punched disconnect. And turned toward her. "All my truck tires are flat."

"What? All of them? That's ridiculous. No one has four flat tires."

He raised an eyebrow, but before he could say anything she clued in. "Oh, someone did it deliberately."

He nodded.

"But why?"

"That's a darn good question." He frowned and was silent for a moment. "I can't think of a single person who would do this, can you?"

She tapped her lip as she tried to think or a possibility, then shook her head. "No. I can't. Did you piss someone off recently?"

"Not that I can think of. Do you have an old flame that would be jealous?"

She laughed at that, she hadn't even been out on a date in over a year. "No. I don't have all that many old flames. Do you have one that would be pissed to see your truck at my place all night long?"

He ran his fingers through his hair and pulled on it. "No. All my most recent girlfriends are married or moved away."

"It's a definite malicious attack. So, if it's not an old flame of yours or mine, who else could it be."

"I can't think of anyone I might have pissed off lately, other than those two guys that attacked you, and they're still locked up in the city jail, waiting for whoever won the coin toss to prosecute them first."

She looked at her window then back at Chase. "Do you think it has something to do with my window? It's been over a week, but we don't normally have these types of crimes in our town."

He looked at the window too. "It does seem to be a little coincidental. We'll see what Drake says, he's on duty this morning as is my brother. I'm sure they'll have plenty to say about it."

She nodded. "Most definitely." She looked around the store. "Even though I don't have any customers, I should probably stay in here. The pharmacy doesn't open for another hour. Once Drake and Drew give you the scoop, will you come back in and tell me what they said? Oh, and I have an air compressor in the shed out back you can use to re-inflate your tires providing they didn't slash them. Did they?"

"No. I didn't see any damage, so they must have just let the air out. That would have taken a long time, those are big tires. So, whoever it is must be a very patient person."

"Or have nothing to do."

CHASE WALKED BACK OUT to his truck just as two black SUV's with stripes and decals that proclaimed them as official vehicles, drove up. Drake climbed out of one and his brother Drew got out of the other one.

Drake walked over and around Chase's truck while Drew started asking questions. The questions were asked in a police capacity, but he still felt like some of the information was private.

Yes, he'd spent the night at Katie's. No, they didn't hear anything. No, he hadn't pissed anyone off. No, they couldn't think of anyone who would do this. He didn't like voicing the exact hours he'd been here with her. It wasn't anyone else's business but the two of them. But this prank now brought more attention to their private lives than he wanted. And that was more irritating than the actual act.

Drake came over to them, nodded to Drew who went over to look carefully at the truck tires and the area around them. "I don't see any damage."

Chase put his hands on his hips. "No, I didn't either. I could have just pumped them up with Katie's air compressor, but with her window getting broken last week, and now this. I figured you would want to know."

Drake nodded. "You figured correctly."

"Those guys are still locked up correct?"

He nodded. "Yes, they are so, it can't be them."

"I suppose not but it all seems to be too coincidental that both Katie's window got busted and now my tires are flat since those guys went to jail."

"I don't believe in coincidences. But I can't put them here doing this, unless they have a third guy we don't know about."

A third guy? Now that was an interesting idea, but if there was a third guy, why would he stick around. His friends were not nice men and he could go to jail for being an accomplice. Chase was certain that if it was him, he'd have been on the road within the hour of the police taking the guys to jail. "That's an idea I hadn't thought about. Guess that's why you're the Sheriff and I'm a cowboy."

Drake guffawed. "Not that it's doing a lot of good. I have no idea where to look for someone. With them not doing any real damage to your truck this is more of a nuisance report, but it might all go together in the end, so I'm glad you called."

"I hope it does some good. Now I better get my tires filled up and get home. I have work to do today."

"Chase, if you're not going to spend the night tonight you might want to try to convince Katie to go with you out to the ranch. I still don't like her being alone here at night with these things going on. If it was a normal neighborhood it would be one thing. But she's all alone on Main street. George has living quarters above the bar, but that's all the way down the street."

Chase nodded. "I hear you and I will do my best. She's a stubborn woman."

Drake grinned. "That she is."

Chase filled up his tires and then went inside to tell Katie what Drake had said. He tried to convince her to come out to the ranch tonight, but this was her late night keeping the store open, so she said she didn't think she would feel up to driving out after she'd worked twelve hours.

She shook her head at his expression. "And no, I don't think I'll have the energy to entertain you here. I'll be fine. I'll call someone if I hear anything."

He couldn't think of anything else to say so he gave her a long hot kiss. "If you change your mind call me, and I'll come running."

She looked a little dazed but nodded her head.

He grinned and walked out the door. He had a full day's work to do, too.

CHAPTER 22

*K*atie thought about the flat tires and her broken window and what Drake had said about a third person all morning, while she went about the day's work. It seemed pretty far-fetched to her. Even if there had been a third person, why would they still be hanging around? She also couldn't imagine sitting out in the dark for hours to let the air out of all his tires. Who had that kind of patience? Cutting off the valve stems would do the job and be faster. Plus, it was less likely to get caught that way. Not that a lot of people went out into her back area, and it wasn't visible from the street. But people did use the alley and Chase might not have spent the night. It was just plain odd.

When Gwen came in for her short work shift she looked tired. She was still mostly clean from her bath yesterday except her hands were dirty.

"Good morning Gwen. Oh, I didn't have time for laundry last night a friend stopped by and then I kind of forgot about it. I'll get them back to you tomorrow."

Gwen looked at the floor as she answered. "That's okay I've got these that you gave me for now."

135

"I'll get them to you tomorrow. Did you finish the shelves yesterday?"

Gwen still didn't meet her eyes. "Not quite, I have two more to go."

"When you get them done, let me know."

Gwen walked off still without looking at her, which seemed kind of odd. Usually she looked right at her but didn't talk much. She'd talked more today but wouldn't look at her. Some customers came in, so she didn't have time to dwell on it.

When lunch time rolled around Katie thought she might be able to get Gwen to talk over fried chicken, all kids liked chicken, didn't they? When she had the food in her hand she called out to Gwen. "I got a bucket of chicken with all the fixin's for lunch, come eat." She saw Gwen look up quickly and then she looked back down just as fast. But she did start walking toward the break room.

She got some plates, napkins, and plastic silverware out while Gwen washed her hands. When she sat at the table Katie noticed her hands still looked dirty, almost like they were stained.

"Would you like a leg, a thigh or a breast?"

The girl looked at her through her lashes and said, "A leg, please."

"Good, are you not feeling well today, you seem a little down."

Gwen wrapped her arms around her waist and her shoulders drooped. "J-just tired."

Katie wasn't sure she believed that, but she wasn't going to argue or push, much.

Loading up Gwen's plate with a leg, a biscuit, mashed potatoes and coleslaw, she then repeated the same process with her own, choosing a breast and said cheerfully, "Maybe the food will help."

She couldn't help but notice that when Gwen took a bite of her chicken leg that her hands were shaking. She waited until Gwen had eaten most of the food on her plate. The girl was eating, but not in her normal youthful fashion. "Gwen honey, it looks more than tired to me, are you sick or hurt?"

She shook her head and pushed her plate away. "I think I should go get some sleep. Thanks for lunch. I'll see you tomorrow."

"Why don't you take some of the leftovers with you and let me pay you for today."

Gwen shook her head. "I'll get it tomorrow." Then she scurried out of the store.

Katie sat back in her chair, *well that was a disaster.* She just couldn't figure out what the problem was. She hadn't really acted tired or sick, or hurt for that matter. But something was wrong, that was for certain. She'd acted almost like Katie was angry with her, but there was no reason why she would be upset. Yesterday they'd had a good afternoon and Gwen had acted excited to be clean. Then Gwen had left right after Chase had walked in.

She remembered the mean look on Gwen's face when she looked at Chase, and then she'd just disappeared. Katie couldn't think of anything Chase had done to upset the girl. He hadn't even looked at her or spoken to her.

Her thoughts turned a new direction and she didn't like it one little bit, but it was about the only thing that made sense. Was it possible Gwen wasn't feeling scared, that she was feeling guilty. Her hands were dirty, and she wouldn't look at Katie. Maybe she was building a mountain out of a molehill but as she thought about it she wondered. Was Gwen the one who had flattened Chase's tires? Tire dirt was almost impossible to wash off your hands, and she might be feeling guilty this morning.

She needed to talk to someone about it, but she wasn't

ready to talk to the Sheriff or Chase. Perhaps she could talk to Summer. She sent Summer a text asking her if she could come by after she closed up the feed store.

CHASE WAS a little disappointed that Katie didn't want to see him later, but he had to admit they very rarely got together on her night to close. In the summer she stayed open until nine or sometimes nine-thirty, if she was busy, and then once she locked the door she still had to close out the register, put the money in the safe and whatever else closing entailed. So, they normally didn't get together, but that's when they'd just been friends. After his first night in her bed he had to admit he would have been happy to have a repeat, even if it was later in the evening.

When he saw Cade the first thing he did was say, "I slept with Katie last night and if you punch me over it I will punch you back."

Cade shrugged. "Yeah, I figured that, when you didn't come home last night. Since it was clearly at her invitation, there is no reason to punch you. It doesn't exactly thrill me to pieces, but if she's happy then I'm good."

"What am I? Chopped liver?"

"I suppose I can be happy for you too. But I will punch you if you hurt her."

"If I hurt her, I'll let you."

"Good to know. We need to get to work. Since you spent all morning with Katie we're behind. I thought you were just going to be a little late."

Chase nodded. "That was the plan. But when I went out to come back all my truck tires were flat."

Cade frowned. "All of them, that's ridiculous no one gets four flats. Unless..."

"Yeah, unless it was deliberate. Which it had to be, but they weren't slashed, or the valve stems cut off. Someone apparently sat there and deflated all of my tires."

"But that would take a lot of time unless they had one of those quick deflate tools people use for off-roading." Cade tipped his head to the side. "I can't imagine sitting there patiently letting the air out of even one tire on a car, let alone all four on a truck, that's a hell of a lot of air even with one of those tools."

"Exactly my thought. I can't figure it out. Anyway, I called Drake and he and Drew came out and did an incident report. Between that and the picture window it seems a little shady to me."

Cade put his hands on his hips. "Did you convince Katie to come back here?"

"Not yet. She has to close tonight, and she said she didn't want to come out or have me sleep over again. But I may not give her that choice. Once we get done here and it starts getting dark I plan to head to town, whether she wants it or not I'm not leaving her alone."

"Good. I could come with you to convince her."

Chase nodded. "I'll think about that."

"Just let me know and I'm there."

"No plans with Tanya tonight?"

Cade crossed his arms. "This and Katie are more important."

"I don't think Tanya would agree."

Cade shrugged.

CHAPTER 23

*S*ummer tripped into Katie's store that evening with a huge grin on her face. She glanced around the store, which was empty, and called out, "I'm here."

Katie laughed at her friend, silly girl, it's not like Katie could miss the fact that Summer had arrived, since Katie was standing less than eight feet from the door. Every time she saw Summer she wondered why the woman played down her assets, she had long blond hair that she kept in a tight bun at the back of her neck. Her bright blue eyes she hid behind glasses that did not suit her face. She had a nice shape that was always camouflaged in bulky clothes and a shop apron. And no makeup, ever. Katie itched to doll her up, instead she shook her head. "Are you sure about that? You might still be outside."

Summer laughed. She had a big laugh, that made it so that a person couldn't help but smile when they heard it. "Yep, here I am as requested. What's the scoop?"

Katie frowned when she thought about why she'd asked Summer to come over that night. "I need an opinion on something and I didn't want it to be from Chase or the Sheriff."

"That sounds ominous."

She couldn't help the big sigh that escaped her, so she nodded. "It is a little bit. And it's going to take a while. Did you eat? I have cold fried chicken in the fridge."

Summer grinned. "I love cold chicken. I would be happy to take a piece or two off your hands. Do you want me to bring you out some?"

"Yeah a thigh. We can talk here at the register in case someone comes in. It's been pretty slow tonight so there probably won't be anyone, but I need to stay open just in case."

"I understand. The hours are clearly written on the door. So, unless there is an emergency it's best to follow them." Summer turned and walked back to the break room.

Katie didn't think what she wanted to talk about was an emergency, but it was kind of a critical discussion, so she hoped no one would come in.

Summer put the paper plates with food down on the counter with two bottles of water. "Okay, enough hedging, spill."

"I think we've got a homeless girl here in town." Summer looked shocked, so Katie continued to tell her everything she'd observed and done, since Gwen had first walked into her store.

"Wow, you're a very generous person, but she's so young, don't you think you should call CPS or something."

Katie felt her stomach drop, she did feel like she should do something but was afraid for Gwen. "Probably, but she was so skittish at first, I was afraid she would run. But now I'm really concerned and that's what I asked you over to talk about."

"Okay, I'm listening."

"This morning, when Chase left to go home—"

"Wait. What? Chase spent the night? Here with you?"

Katie blushed. "Don't tell me you are the only person in town that did not hear about me practically propositioning the man at Karaoke the other night."

"Of course, I heard about it, but I just thought everyone was reading more into a song and a kiss than was warranted. So, you two?" Summer circled her finger in the air.

"Yes, we talked it over and decided to move our relationship up a notch, from best friends, to friends with benefits, even lovers."

"Wow that's very brave of you to risk your forever friendship. Sex changes things, sometimes good and sometimes not so good." Summer shook her head and Katie wondered what the other woman had been through to make such a statement.

"We made a pact. That regardless of how things turned out we were still going to be friends."

Summer grimaced. "I hope you guys are strong enough to do that, if things go south."

"I'm hoping they don't go wrong, but anyway, back to Gwen."

"Oh, right, sorry I interrupted, but this is kind of a huge deal, you and Chase. Wow." She tapped her chin and just looked at Katie.

"I suppose, but I need you to focus. This is important."

Summer shook her head like a dog. "Fine. I'm ready."

Katie explained about the tires and then told Summer how Gwen had acted completely different from her normal self. When she finished speaking she just waited for Summer to speak.

"Hmm, skittish, wouldn't look at you, hands shaking and dirty, didn't wait for her pay. Sounds like guilt to me."

With a huge sigh, Katie said, "Darn it, that's what I

thought too. But why would she do that. She doesn't know Chase."

"Was she jealous? Do you think?"

"I don't think so, she started glaring at him from the moment he walked in. Before he even talked to me."

"That's odd, why would she do that? It's not like he's in town all the time. How could he make anyone mad at him when he spends all his time on the Rockin' K. He was in town to fix your window. And of course, the night you were accosted he punched those guys. But what would that have to do with Gwen, you hadn't met her yet, had you?"

"No, I didn't meet her until a couple of days after the window was broken." Katie thought back to the day of the attack. Now that she was far enough away from it she could think about it more clearly. The guys had come into the store to pick up a few things and had been trying to come onto her even then, but she'd ignored them and rung up their purchases. Beer, jerky, chips, three frozen dinners, wait three... and a pink lemonade frozen drink, for their little sister. Well, hell.

"Those guys—" the door chimed, and she stopped speaking until Chase walked in. "Chase, I just remembered. Summer, Chase, those guys that attacked me, they have a sister. A younger sister."

Summer gasped and whispered, "Gwen."

Katie nodded and grabbed Summer's hand. "Exactly. We have to do something."

Chase frowned. "What do you mean we have to do something? Who's Gwen? And why do we care?"

"Gwen is those guys' little sister, she's about eleven. She's been in here homeless and hungry, so I've been paying her to help me with some things and feeding her lunch and letting her take a bath and stuff. She flattened your tires and was probably the one who broke the window. We have to help her!"

Chase's face had turned red. "Help her? We need to arrest her. She's a juvenile delinquent."

"No, I don't think so. I think she's scared and yeah, pissed off. But she doesn't know what to do, we have to help her."

Chase crossed his arms. "Explain to me why we have to help her instead of calling the Sheriff and CPS."

Katie told the whole story to Chase who still didn't look convinced, but he did look a little less inclined to call the Sheriff.

CHASE COULD NOT BELIEVE his ears. There was a homeless girl Katie was feeding and paying to work in her store. Was she nuts? But he had to admit her reasoning about suspecting the girl as the window and tire culprit made good sense. What she thought they should do about it was completely insane. In his book, they needed to call CPS and the Sheriff and be done with it. Although whether they could find her was the real issue.

He was thinking fast while Katie tried to convince him they should help the girl. If he let her wait until tomorrow when Gwen came into work for her, they could surround her in the store, if he got the Sheriff and a brother or two involved. Katie only had two doors for customers and then her back door for deliveries from the alley. So maybe all they really needed was him and Drake and whoever else was on duty tomorrow. He couldn't remember if Drew was going to be on tomorrow. But even if he wasn't he could talk to him about all this tonight and see what he advised.

It was clear however, that Katie was not in any danger. The kid wasn't going to bite the hand that was feeding her and even her letting the air out of his tires was pretty harmless. The broken window had been from her first reaction, when she was most likely terrified and angry to have her brothers taken into custody.

He decided he would not try to convince Katie to turn the girl in. She might dig in her heels. He knew what needed to happen and he would just take care of everything. Then Katie wouldn't have anything to worry or feel guilty about. She was a soft-hearted woman and was thinking with her heart, not her head.

When Katie wound down. He asked, "What makes you think Gwen will take your help? Won't she just run off?"

"I think she's desperate enough to take it. With it still being Indian summer she's fine, but once winter rolls around it will be another story all together. I'll explain that to her."

He and Summer both nodded, but he still wasn't convinced. "I think that we should make sure she can't leave the building until you have a chance to talk her into telling you the truth. I could get a couple of guys to hang by your doors and just make sure she doesn't try to run."

Katie nodded. "Yeah some of your brothers or a ranch hand would come in handy to watch the doors."

He rubbed his chin still thinking. "Sounds good. What time would be good?"

"Lunch time might be best. That way I'll have the time to sit down with her and talk it out, plus we'll be in the break room."

Chase nodded, that would be good. He'd round up some guys to help with the operation. "I'll get going then, so I can make some calls and you can lock up."

Katie smiled and then gave him a warm kiss, right in front of Summer, who looked a little shocked.

He grinned at her. "Might as well get used to it."

CHAPTER 24

*K*atie paced back and forth, she was a nervous wreck, and had been all morning. If she was honest she'd been that way all night too, tossing and turning, punching her pillow. She kept going over and over what she should say. Thinking about how to get the girl to level with her and tell her the truth. Katie wanted Gwen to know she wasn't still angry about the window. Or the truck tires for that matter. The thought of that child not having anywhere to go, when the temperatures started to drop, was frightening.

When Gwen finally came into the store looking a little more relaxed, Katie was able to calm down too.

"Good morning, Gwen. I'd like you to straighten up the toy section and make a list of anything that needs restocking. Actually, please make a list of everything you find back there, so we can make some decisions for next year. It's changing of the seasons time so an inventory of everything would be good."

The girl nodded and took the pen and notepad and went back to the children's section. Katie kept a lot of games, card decks and simple toys. People on vacation often didn't think about what to do in the evenings or as a family. As they put their normal activities on hold for a few days they often looked for a family game. She sold many decks of "Old Maid" and "Crazy Eights" and lots of games. Summer was over, which made it a perfect time to take stock and prepare for next year.

While Gwen worked on the children's area Katie assessed the jewelry. A lot of what she had was turquoise, Black Hills Gold and the ever-popular aspen leaf, that looked like it was dipped in gold or silver. She also carried a few really nice pieces from Colorado jewelry designers. One of her favorites was a woman in southern Colorado that created very unique items. She needed to call her to put in an order and send her the payment for what she'd sold the previous quarter.

Katie didn't wear a lot of jewelry, but she always loved looking at it and working with the artists to have something new and fun for her store. The local women waited for new items to arrive and then swarmed the place. Katie took notes on what she needed, and what she might want to send back because she had too much of it. She could also put it on sale. Maybe she would put it on sale first and then see what she had left that she might want to send back. Sometimes a piece she thought would sell quickly didn't, at least not at *her* store, and it was possible that it would sell better somewhere else. Better to move it along than have it sit in her display case getting dusty.

Gwen came up front just as Katie was finishing with the jewelry and handed Katie the list she'd made.

Gwen smiled. "Lots of toys."

Katie showed her the list she'd made. "And lots of jewelry, too."

Gwen looked at the similarly long list and nodded.

"Let's have some lunch. I whipped us up a fancy salad this

morning." She didn't mention that she'd done it very, very, early this morning. Because she couldn't sleep and couldn't stand to be in bed any longer.

Katie followed Gwen into the break room and got out the food and drinks she had ready, her hands were shaking she was so nervous. She put everything on the table and encouraged Gwen to sit down to eat. After Gwen had eaten most of her salad and Katie had pushed hers around on the plate she got up and closed the door.

Gwen looked at her wide-eyed.

"I wanted to talk to you in private." She sat and folded her hands, pushing the food to the side. "We've been working together for a while now, Gwen. You are a very good employee, and I'm happy to have you continue to work with me. Gwen honey, I need you to level with me."

Gwen looked at the door and back at Katie. "What do you mean?"

Katie took one of the girl's hands and noticed they were cold as ice. "I suspect you are homeless, Gwen and that maybe your brothers are the guys that were arrested a while back."

Gwen started to pull her hand away, but Katie held on tight. "It's not your fault. I suspect your brothers are worried about you, too. I would like to reassure them that you're okay and, well, even make sure you stay that way."

Gwen whispered, "How would you do that?"

"I don't know exactly, but I can't help you at all if you don't tell me the truth."

Gwen's eyes filled with tears and Katie's heart broke for the child.

"Let me help you, Gwen."

"They're not always bad. Only when they drink. They kept promising to stop. It's just we've all been confused since our parents died." Her voice hitched. "I've been so scared, and

I miss them. I'm sorry I broke your window, but I was so mad."

"Don't worry about that."

"I saw them talking to you and then you all went into the alley and up against the building, so I couldn't see. Then that guy came and yelled and punched Tommy. I grabbed a wrench Kevin had brought in after working on the car and ran out of the hotel room. I had to wait until the lobby was empty to sneak out, by the time I came around the corner, the police were there. So, I hid."

Gwen scrubbed at her eyes. "Then I couldn't get back in the hotel room. I didn't have a key. All our stuff was in there. I didn't know what to do or where to go, I just hid for a long time. Then later when it was quiet I tried to find a way into the hotel or anywhere that I could sleep. When I couldn't find anywhere I was so mad I hit your window with the wrench"

"The person at the front desk could have let you into your hotel room."

The girl's breath shuddered. "Tommy told me not to tell anyone I was in there, they didn't pay for me."

"Oh sweetie, that wouldn't matter."

Gwen shrank down into herself as she whispered. "Then when I got scared to go back to the grocery store, because the guy there started asking all kinds of questions, I came here. You were so nice to me. I felt bad for breaking your window."

That poor frightened child, how could anyone be angry with her. "I forgive you, Gwen."

"But that guy that hit my brothers, I don't like him, so I let the air out of his tires. Tommy's wrench has a thing for letting air out. We used it when we all used to go off-roading. My parents and me in one car and Tommy and Kevin in another. It was so much fun. Then one night mom and dad went to a movie and never came home." The girl dissolved into wracking sobs.

Katie's heart shattered, and she pulled Gwen into her arms.

When the sobs quieted to hiccups. Katie said, "We'll figure something out. Do you have any other family?"

Before Gwen could say another word, Chase and Sheriff Drake walked into the room. Behind them was a matronly woman that Katie guessed was a CPS worker.

Gwen jumped up and backed further into the room. "You called the cops on me?"

Katie glared at Chase. "No. I didn't. I really do want to help."

"You were just lying to me, my brothers told me not to trust anyone, but them. I should have listened."

"No. Now listen to me, these people want to help you, too." She reached toward Gwen, who moved away and wrapped her arms around herself.

Gwen tried to fight back, when Sheriff Drake and the CPS woman approached her. The two of them easily subdued the frightened girl. She looked at Katie with so much fear and anger battling in her eyes. "I trusted you."

As the officials escorted the girl from the room Katie looked at Chase with tears in her own eyes. "Chase, how could you? I was helping her. I trusted you, Chase, and you betrayed that trust. And me."

CHASE FELT the blood drain from his body, he had never seen so much anger and pain on Katie's face. His heart broke at the feeling of betrayal he could see in her expression. "Katie, honey, the girl needs real help."

She narrowed her eyes at him. "I *was* helping her Chase.

She doesn't need to be hauled to jail or some, some foster home. Or worse. I don't want to discuss it with you. Get out of my store."

She pointed to the door. "Get out. Get out now."

Chase didn't know what to do. He'd only been trying to help. Katie couldn't keep taking care of a homeless girl. The authorities needed to be brought in to handle this. But he guessed he'd done it all wrong. He should have tried to convince Katie that the girl needed real help, maybe they could find her family or something.

"Katie, we need to talk about this. You're not her mother or a relative, she needs someone to help her find her family. You know me, you know I wasn't trying to hurt the girl."

Katie looked at him with daggers in her eyes. "Apparently I don't know you at all. I can't believe you could be so insensitive, so heartless. Her parents are dead. What if she doesn't have any other family, or what if they're abusive? You don't know anything about her. I was asking her those kinds of questions. She was talking to me. And now you've sent her away before I can finish."

She pushed past him and went into the store, directly toward the pharmacist, Steven. She talked with him for a minute and then marched out the door. He trailed after her as she charged down the street toward the Sheriff's office.

Chase didn't know what to say or do to convince Katie he wasn't a heartless monster. He hadn't thought about the idea that Gwen's parents might be abusive or dead. All his thoughts had centered on getting the girl back with her family, so Katie wouldn't be consumed by her.

Maybe his actions had been a little self-centered. And he could admit he did kind of consider the girl a bit of a juvenile delinquent. She had broken the window and flattened his tires. Well that's what they thought anyway. He could also acknowledge the girl had looked terrified and very, very young.

He huffed and tried to catch up to Katie. "I'm sorry, I thought I was helping."

She stopped and turned to him. Poking him in the chest she said, "I don't know what in the hell you were doing, but it sure as hell was not helping. And you know it. You deliberately allowed me to believe you were going to let me handle it. You flat out lied to me, Chase Kipling."

"Katie…" he'd never seen the look of disgust that was written across her face and it terrified him. Not physically, but emotionally.

"No. Don't deny it, just go. I can't stand to even look at you right now."

He tried again. "But we can't leave it like this."

"We can, for now. That scared girl needs me, not you. I'm the only person she knows in the whole town and I am not going to let her down."

She turned her back on him and left him standing there. His heart broke and he couldn't breathe, it hurt so much. He realized right then, just how much he loved her. Now that he'd quite possibly screwed everything up.

CHAPTER 25

Katie stormed into the Sheriff's office. She couldn't think about what Chase had done, because she might collapse into a puddle of sorrow. How could she have known him for twenty years and had no idea what a jerk he could be? She couldn't think about that, so instead, she held onto her righteous anger at his betrayal, and the fact that Gwen needed her. Anger and a mission, were much better than the pain of losing her best friend.

The CPS woman and Sheriff Drake were sitting in his office talking. Drew was just getting ready to go out on patrol. She didn't see Gwen anywhere. "Drew, where is Gwen?"

"In back with her brothers."

Katie screeched, "You locked up a child? Have you lost your minds? Is that even legal?"

Drew took her arm and said soothingly, "No Katie, we didn't lock up a child. She begged us to let her see her brothers and Drake and Mrs. Armstrong agreed that would be acceptable."

"Oh, well I guess she would want to see them. That was nice of you."

Drake came out of his office. "Katie, please come in here, we need to ask you some questions."

Katie didn't want to spend hours talking to Drake, she needed to see Gwen. "I want to see Gwen and make sure she's all right."

"You can do that after the questions," Drake said.

She knew the Sheriff would get his way, so she resigned herself to the inquisition. The sooner it was over, the sooner she could see Gwen.

She told Drake every little detail she knew about Gwen. And explained five times, why she hadn't called him or CPS to help take care of the girl. Both of them had stressed to her how badly things could have gone, by her choosing the path she had taken. She realized she had been foolish to try to handle it alone.

After what seemed like hours, they finally let her into the back to see Gwen.

She walked to the cell where the three of them were, to find Gwen fast asleep on the bunk, with her head in one brother's lap and the other brother sitting on the floor holding her hand.

The brothers looked up at her as she approached, but instead of seeing animosity in their eyes, she saw gratitude.

The one on the floor cleared his throat. "We want to apologize for attacking you. Landing in this jail has been a real wakeup call for us."

The one on the bunk spoke up. "We can't thank you enough for looking after our sister. The fear and worry we've felt for her, while we've been locked up in here, brought home to us what's really important in life."

The one on the floor shook his head. "Our sister is more important than having a good time, drinking and taking advantage of women. We were fools to put her into jeopardy like that."

The one on the bunk ran his hand down Gwen's hair. "Our parents would skin us alive if they were still here to see it. I'm so ashamed of risking Gwen, by living inside a bottle the last few months. Yes, it dulled the pain of our parents' deaths."

"But that is nothing to the pain we'd have felt if something had happened to Gwen." The one on the floor hung his head in shame.

Katie looked at the sleeping girl. "She's a good girl and the way I hear it, you two are not going to be out of jail for some time. Even before you stand trial for your past acts. Which one of you is Tommy?"

The one on the bunk winced at the name and rubbed the back of his neck. "Me. You're right, we're mean drunks. We deserve what we get, but Gwen doesn't."

"No, she doesn't. And you might want to think about how you would feel if some drunk guys treated your sister like you did me."

Kevin gasped. "It would kill me to have her go through that. I'm so damned sorry we treated you that way."

Tommy nodded. "We were fools, we've sure as hell learned our lesson. I just hope Gwen will be all right."

Katie wondered if there was something she could do. She left the three of them, Gwen was at peace with her brothers and now that they were sober, they almost seemed like nice guys. It was too bad they had made the choices they had.

CHASE DROVE HOME IN A FOG, his mind whirled non-stop, trying to find a way out of the mess he'd just put himself into. He couldn't bear to lose Katie. He needed someone to talk to.

Cade was out with Tanya, so it wouldn't be him. Maybe his dad or mom, or even better, Grandpa K, they were all older and wiser and that's exactly what he needed. His older brothers would do in a pinch, or their women.

He found his grandfather in the kitchen and sighed with relief. "Thank God you're here, Grandpa K, I need some advice."

Grandpa K lifted his coffee cup. "I might have some of that on me."

"Good, because I really screwed the pooch this time." Chase ran his fingers through his hair and tugged, he didn't know where to start. He didn't know if his grandfather knew he was dating Katie let alone how far it had progressed. He paced around the kitchen trying to decide what to say.

His grandfather sat patiently and waited while he waged an internal war. When Chase finally decided how to start he turned toward his grandpa.

But before he could say anything, Grandpa K said, "Nothing upsets a man's equilibrium more than messing up a good relationship with his woman. Sit down and tell me what you did to upset Katie."

Thank God, he didn't have to go into all the basics. How his grandpa knew everything, he didn't know, but he wasn't about to look a gift horse in the mouth. "She thinks I betrayed her, and in a way, I guess I did."

His grandfather raised his eyebrows and motioned Chase to go on. He started talking and got every bit of it off his chest. He talked until he ran out of breath and then kept talking. He'd never talked so much in his life.

While he spewed all over the room, Grandpa K listened.

When he finally ran out of words he got a glass of water and drank the whole thing down to ease the dryness and ache in his throat.

"Yep, you surely did dive headfirst into a pile of manure, son."

Chase barked out a laugh. "That's a very apt way to put it. So, what should I do?"

"You know the girl better than anyone. Start up a campaign to convince her you understand. Are sorry. And won't do anything like it again."

"So, send her flowers or something?" Chase asked.

"Flowers never hurt, but I don't think any one thing is going to magically make everything better. Don't be a cliché. Think about who Katie is, what she loves, what you like to do together, and appeal to that knowledge of her. I assume you're in this with her for the long haul?"

Chase nodded as his heart clenched. "Yes, I didn't realize until she was so mad at me, but I love her."

"You've loved her for a long time."

"Yes, as a best friend. But I discovered I'm also *in love* with her. I want to spend the rest of my life with her as my best friend, and my wife."

"In that case make sure she knows that. Show her how a life with you will be. It's almost always about communication. Talk to her Chase… after you soften her up some."

"Thanks Grandpa, I think I'll take my horse out for a ride, so I can plot and plan."

"You do that. And check on the southern fences as you ride."

Chase chuckled. "Will do. Might as well be productive at the same time."

"Sometimes a man thinks best when his hands are busy."

Grandpa K stood up from the table and Chase wrapped him in a fierce hug. "Thanks."

"It'll work out, son. Katie's a fine woman and she'll forgive you eventually."

Chase grabbed some tools, saddled his horse and went

157

out to ride, his thoughts on Katie, and how much he'd hurt her and what he could do to fix it. He had to fix it, she was too important to him. As he rode he thought back over their lives together and came up with a plan of attack. When he ventured upon a section of fence with some barbed wire that had broken and curled back on itself it gave him an idea. The fence would hold up, but it would need some new wire strung so he marked the location for later.

When he got back to the house he went straight to his room, to start on his campaign to win Katie back. A couple of hours later his brother walked in.

"You missed dinner. Mom sent you a plate," Cade said as he kicked the door closed behind him and looked around for a clear surface to set the tray.

Chase groaned as he straightened up from his hunched position. Every joint cracked and popped and his muscles strained as they stretched. He gathered up his drawings that were scattered across the desk, his stomach growling at the scent of food, Cade had brought in with him.

"What is all this?" Cade asked.

"My campaign to win Katie back."

His brother set the tray down on the newly cleared surface and put his hands on his hips. "What did you do to Katie? It's only been a couple of days. How could you fuck it up so quickly?"

"Have a seat and I'll explain while I eat." As he dug into the Salisbury steak and mashed potatoes, he told his brother about the last twenty-four hours.

Cade listened and nodded with an occasional grimace thrown in. "I can't say I wouldn't have done the same thing, because I probably would have, but I can see why Katie would be pissed. She never did like us railroading her into something."

All the food Chase had just eaten turned to lead at his brother's words.

"So, what is your plan to convince the woman you aren't as big of an idiot as she now thinks you are?"

As Chase explained his plan, his brother offered suggestions and refinements on the campaign. When Chase took his plate down to the kitchen, several hours later, he finally felt he had a slim chance at winning her back. His heart didn't hurt quite so much and there was a glimmer of hope peeking through the gloom.

CHAPTER 26

*K*atie found a large manila envelope taped to her front door the next morning, when she went down to open her store. It had Chase's handwriting on it and she was tempted to tear it up and throw it away without even looking at it. But her curiosity was too great, she always marveled at people that had the strength to toss something without looking at it first.

She laid the envelope on the counter and went through her morning opening routine before she went back and opened the envelope. She pulled out the sheaf of papers that were stapled together to form a book. It was a story about a Superman that looked a lot like Chase.

It was a chronicle of their lives together and every time he came to her rescue. Starting when they were little kids and he and Cade had stood up for her, when the class bully had picked on her in the first grade. Some of the pages showed her as Wonder Woman helping one of them.

It was an amusing book, and she felt herself smiling as she came to the end. Then her smile faded when they got to Gwen. He'd drawn himself thinking of Gwen as a fire breathing dragon, but in the reality of the situation she was drawn as a frightened rabbit and he was standing with a sword at her throat.

When Katie turned the page, Chase was on his knees begging both her and Gwen for forgiveness, with his superman cape locked in a chest. He looked so sad she wanted to cry.

She slipped the book under the counter when she heard the door chime, signaling a customer.

CHASE WAS EXHAUSTED, he'd spent the whole day in town, and making calls. The first thing he'd done was gone to the Sheriff's office to talk to Drake. Then he'd talked to Gwen's brothers. After that he'd spent the rest of the day on the phone.

When he finally finished with all the calls, he decided that ranching was a whole hell of a lot easier than what he'd spent the day doing. But all of this was for Katie and he couldn't think of a worthier cause, and if it was uncomfortable and awkward, well, it was no less than he deserved.

He still didn't feel like what he did was wrong, and even more so after talking to her brothers. He shuddered to think of them going to jail and leaving their sister to fend for herself. Living on the streets might be safe in their town, but once the temperatures dropped here that would be a whole other story.

This way she was getting the help she needed. Her brothers had been on the way to Nebraska to take her to their Aunt Mary. They'd not told Gwen that, because they weren't sure how she would react, and they hadn't decided if they wanted to live there. They'd only met their aunt a few times, her and her husband were cattle ranchers and they didn't leave their home very often. The will that was read after their parents' death had very clearly left custody of Gwen to Aunt Mary. So, they were taking her there, just not very quickly.

Next on his *win back Katie* campaign was a trip into Denver. He needed to visit a jewelry store and not just any store but one that carried the jewelry from her favorite designer. He'd called the designer earlier today and she'd told him where to find what he wanted. Then he'd called the store and asked them to hold it for him.

When he got a text from Drew, he decided he might as well do that drive today. So, he'd be out of the house tonight. He wasn't giving up however, he would win her back, he just hoped it was sooner rather than later.

KATIE WAS ITCHING to go to the Sheriff's office, she wanted to find out what was happening with Gwen. She'd thought she could slip out at lunch time and leave the store in the hands of her pharmacist Steven, but a whole family of tourists had swarmed her store and wanted help with everything. From first aid cream to what souvenirs would be best for the hundreds of friends and family they were taking things back for. She'd barely squeezed in a couple bites of her lunch. Then Steven had taken his lunch, and she'd been busy all the rest of the afternoon. This was the strangest Wednesday on record, with so many people coming in.

Summer rushed in her door in the late afternoon. "I heard through the grapevine that Chase was an idiot."

"Yes, he brought Drake and CPS." Even saying it out loud to Summer hurt. How could he do something like that? She just didn't understand how he could betray her like he did, with no thought to her feelings.

"Not exactly what we planned. I wanted to get here earlier, but the tourists today…."

"You too? I've been wanting to go talk to Drake for hours to check on Gwen, but have been swamped every second of the day."

"Yeah it was crazy. I mean I sell hardware and dog food, what were they doing in my place? At least you have things people on vacation might want."

"You have some handy items, too. But can I ask you a huge favor? Could you stand right here behind the counter while I run down the street to find out about Gwen?"

"Sure, I can do that." Summer nodded.

"Steven can help you if needed."

Summer waved toward the door. "No problem. Go. I can stall them if they need your expertise."

Katie rushed down the street and slammed in the door of the Sheriff's office.

Drew looked up from some paperwork he was doing. "Katie, what's wrong?"

She bent over to catch her breath, she lived at this altitude, but it could still take a toll. "Nothing is wrong." She puffed out, "I've just been too busy. I wanted to check on Gwen."

"Oh, she was here earlier and is now in emergency foster care—"

Katie interrupted him, her temper exploding. "What! She's gone already? She can't be gone. I need to know she's okay. Dammit, Drew. Where is Drake? I need to give him a piece of my mind."

"Katie now calm down—"

"Calm down?" she screeched. "Are you kidding me, it's only been twenty-four hours and now I won't ever see her again."

"Katie." Drew said firmly, much harsher than he'd ever spoken to her.

She frowned, but let him speak.

"You can see her any time you like. She's in emergency foster care at the Rockin' K."

Katie shook her head, sure she was hearing things. "The Rockin' K?"

Drew nodded. "Yes. Mom and dad got emergency foster creds when we were little, and they never allowed them to expire. So, when Drew and Mrs. Armstrong wanted to keep Gwen close to her brothers, mom and dad fit the bill."

Katie just stared at him trying to get her brain to compute what he'd just told her. She did remember a time or two when there had been a strange child staying with the Kipling's for a couple of weeks, but she'd never put two and two together.

"Gwen's Aunt Mary is on her way from Nebraska to take custody of Gwen full time." He shifted from foot to foot. "Her brothers will stand trial, but Chase arranged for them to have a lawyer. And a counselor to help them with their grief and their alcohol addiction."

"Chase?"

"Yes, he came in and talked to them this morning. The lawyer was in earlier, looking through the info Drake got from the other states and talking to them. It seems like the biggest and worse thing they did was take their sister across state lines. It was reported as kidnapping, since they didn't get custody of her in the will."

"But…"

"Yeah, the lawyer says he can make a case against that, since they were headed on a more or less straight line from Bakersfield, California to North Platt, Nebraska. Most of their other crimes were petty and they might get off with restitution and a short jail sentence. While they were out bent on their own destruction, their family almond orchard and home sold. They have a very nice chunk of change waiting for them to collect, which would easily pay all the restitution."

Katie laughed. "So, if they hadn't been idiots…."

"Yeah, they'd have been fine, all three of them. Still probably will be. With some counseling and a good lawyer. The counselor is in there now with them."

Katie sighed. "I'm so relieved. I want to see Gwen, but I'd rather not see your brother quite yet. I'm not ready to forgive him for deceiving me."

"Yeah, but it did work out for the best." He shrugged.

"It does seem that way, but that still doesn't excuse the lying."

"I suppose not. I can work something out to let you see Gwen without Chase around. I'll text you."

"Thanks. I need to get back to work now. I left Summer manning the fort." She hurried out the door, her mind filled with all Chase had done today. It did seem like he had Gwen and her brothers' best interest at heart.

When she got back to her store, the entire counter was filled with a huge bouquet of tulips in every color. Katie could barely see Summer behind them.

Summer grinned at her as she peeked around the flowers. "They're from Chase I assume. He didn't go with the standard roses either, but your favorite flower. Where do you suppose he got tulips in the fall?"

Katie shook her head feeling overwhelmed by Chase's actions. "He seems very determined. I'm guessing they cost him a fortune since they're off season. Wait until I tell you what else he's been up to today."

Katie reiterated for Summer all she'd learned in her few minutes out of the store, and then showed her the book Chase had left for her this morning. When she finished talking, she got a text from Drew saying Chase would be out of the house until at least eight that evening. And for her to come out any time.

Summer sighed after she saw the text. "He really is trying."

Katie nodded and felt herself weakening. "He is but this is a major thing and it can't be swept aside with some flowers and helpfulness."

"No, you definitely need to make him suffer a few more days at least. And even then, he better come up with some pretty powerful promises."

Katie raised a brow. "Like to never lie to me again?"

Summer pointed at her. "That would be a good start."

.

CHAPTER 27

As Katie parked her car at the Rockin' K she realized her hands were shaking, and her stomach was in knots. It was a strange sensation to feel nervous about arriving at a place that was her second home, but she was. It wasn't about seeing Chase, because she knew he would honor her request of being gone when she came to see Gwen.

No, the fear came from how everyone else would treat her. Should she knock on the door? Or just walk in like she'd done for years? She'd brought candy like she always did, but then second guessed herself on that too. Would they want it? Should she leave it in the car? No, it was still daylight and would melt in the heat.

She opened the door, stood, and wiped her sweaty palms on her jeans before opening the back door to retrieve the bags of candy. When Tony slammed out of the house yelling her name in joyful exuberance she nearly cried in relief. Emma followed her son out the door and gave Katie a big hug, once Tony was finished.

Emma whispered, "You, with or without your candy, are

always welcome. We're all on your side. Chase needs to learn a few things. I love him, but he's not always correct in his actions."

Katie choked back the tears that threatened. "Thanks, I was a little nervous."

Gwen came out of the house next, and walked right into Katie's arms for a hug, too. "I'm sorry I yelled at you. Chase explained all about how you had asked him to help, and he'd lied to you about his plans. Plus, I got to see my brothers, so I'm kinda glad he lied to you."

Emma took the candy and her son into the house.

Katie smiled at the girl. "Things do seem to be working out better than I could have predicted. Are you happy here with the Kipling's?"

Gwen nodded. "They are so nice, they got all my stuff from the hotel and gave me a pretty room to sleep in. Chase is helping my brothers, too. He really is a nice guy, I suppose."

"Most of the time he is." Katie had to admit it, but then she remembered his actions from yesterday and frowned. "But lying to me is where I draw the line."

Gwen whispered, "I lied to you too."

Katie's shoulders sagged, and her heart broke for the girl. "Oh sweetie, you were just trying to protect yourself. It's not the same."

"No. But Chase was trying to protect you."

Katie sighed, out of the mouth of babes. "Let's go in and see if Emma needs help with the candy. Then we can talk."

Gwen invited Katie to see her room. Not that she hadn't seen the guest room a million times before, and even slept in it on more than one occasion, but she was pleased that Gwen wanted her in her private space. Apparently, Rachel had moved in with Adam, since Katie had spent the night here on the ranch, was it only eleven days ago?

She spent a pleasant hour and a half, with Gwen talking a mile a minute. Katie was relieved to see that Gwen was a normal eleven-year-old and had been reticent, only so she didn't have to lie. She told Katie all about her former life before her parents had been killed in a car accident. Then about their trek across the states, stopping whenever they got a whim and staying for a few nights. She apparently hadn't known her brothers were stealing to keep them going, and she'd seen it all as a grand adventure. Although she didn't like it when her brothers drank too much, because it made them cranky.

When Gwen finally ran out of words, Katie realized it was nearly eight thirty and she'd been stalling in hopes of seeing Chase. That was just the opposite of how she wanted to feel, so she gave Gwen a hug and told her she would see her soon. And if she wanted to, Gwen was welcome at the store any time, to work or just to hang out.

Gwen said she would ask about that, and gave Katie her cell number. Katie saved it in her phone and sent Gwen a text, so she would have her number too. When she walked out to her car she had the feeling of being watched, but when she looked around she couldn't see anything or anyone.

CHASE WATCHED Katie get in her car and knew she'd felt him watching, but he just couldn't help himself. He had to see her. When he'd arrived home, and had seen Katie's car in the driveway he'd been tempted to go to her. But he'd promised Drew, to let her have time with Gwen without him being around, so he'd parked his truck behind the barn and had climbed up on the roof to wait for her to leave. It gave him an excellent view of the driveway, but no one ever looked up, even if they felt someone watching them.

God, he hoped he could work this out with her because it was flat out going to kill him, if he couldn't get her to forgive him and give him a second chance. He didn't realize quite how much she meant to him until he was persona non grata.

He watched her car drive off getting smaller and smaller until it was gone and then continued staring at the spot where it had disappeared. When he finally climbed down off the roof he found Drew waiting.

"I figured you were lurking out here somewhere," Drew said.

"Yeah, I wanted to come in, but I'd promised you, so I stayed out here. I couldn't resist getting a glimpse of her."

"You've got it bad, don't you?" his brother asked.

Chase pushed on the center of his chest where his heart ached. "Yep, and I've got to get it fixed."

"She was impressed with what you've done so far, and I clearly told her you would only be gone until eight. It's after eight thirty, so it's possible you can take that as a sign that she wouldn't have minded bumping into you."

"Do you think so?" His heart throbbed as that tiny bit of light pierced the darkness and fear he'd been living with.

"Yes, I do, so don't give up hope, big brother, you haven't lost yet, and she's been your friend for twenty years. That's got to count for something."

"Thanks, Drew. I needed to hear that. Now I'm going to go see if I can get Emma and Tony to implement the plan for tomorrow. I thought I would ask them to take my next peace offering into town."

"Tony is cute, but you might think about having Gwen do it. She told me Katie invited her to come into the store, just to hang out or go back to working for her. Gwen doesn't want to just sit around worrying, so she asked me if she could go into town with me in the morning. As long as mom and dad think it's fine, which I can't imagine they wouldn't, she might be your best bet."

Gwen take his things to Katie? Since all the problems focused around his actions concerning her that might work even better. If it looked like Gwen was on his side it might help Katie to soften toward him even more. He felt giddy at the idea. "That's not a bad suggestion. I'll ask her what she thinks. Can you go ask mom and dad in the meantime?"

"Happy to."

Chase felt lighter as he went to the guest room to talk to Gwen. Maybe, just maybe, he could pull this off.

CHAPTER 28

*K*atie was thrilled to see Gwen walk into her store the next day. She had a backpack with her and she looked so hopeful and happy. It was so good to see the girl looking like a normal pre-teen, rather than a fearful one.

"Travis and Meg said I could come spend a few hours with you. I'm happy to work if you have things for me to do. I'm hoping to save up a little money before I go with my aunt. Now that I don't have to spend every cent on food and stuff it will be fun to work."

"You're a very good worker and I'm happy to pay you. The store hasn't been this clean and organized in a good long while. I may have to find someone to take your place when you leave. I didn't realize how messy it had gotten until you started making everything so nice."

"So, you weren't really hiring me for a job."

Katie startled at how much she'd let her guard down. "Um, well, I suppose it was in the back of my mind."

Gwen grinned at her. "No, it wasn't, you made it all up to take care of me, didn't you?"

"Maybe at first, but then I did notice how good everything looked."

Gwen rushed over and hugged her tight. "Thanks so much. I was so scared that first day I came in. And so hungry," she whispered.

Katie's heart cracked in two for this poor girl. "Oh, Gwen, sweetheart, I'm so sorry you had to go through all that."

"It was good for my brother's though. They were getting worse and worse, so I prayed to God to help them. I didn't much like the way he answered that. But it seems to be working, now."

"Yes, it does."

"Oh, and I hope everything works out for you and Chase, too. He sent you something with me this morning." Gwen looked intently at her. "He really is a nice guy and I think you should give him another chance."

Katie frowned. "Did he tell you to say that?"

"No, but he looks so sad." She dug a prettily-wrapped package out of her backpack.

Katie looked down at the box wrapped in her favorite colored paper and sighed. Gwen handed her the homemade card Chase had made, which was a picture of Dolly looking so sad and depressed. Inside it said, "Dolly misses you and so do I." And it had a drawing of Chase and Dolly sitting side by side propping each other up. Both their faces had identical sorrowful expressions.

She shook her head and opened the package. Inside was a bracelet from her favorite jewelry designer. It was one she'd had in her store for a while and she'd loved it, but hadn't had the money to buy it.

Gwen gasped. "It's so beautiful."

"Yes. I loved it. I tried to sell it in here, but no one bought it, so I sent it back to the jewelry designer a few months ago so she could place it somewhere else. I didn't know Chase even knew about it. He pays more attention than I thought."

"Are you going to put it on? Are you going to forgive him?"

"Yes, and probably." She lifted the bracelet out of the box and placed it over her wrist, it sparkled there.

"Someone so caring needs a second chance. Here let me help you." Gwen took the two ends and clasped them together. "His way of doing things is working out better than I could have imagined. I was angry at first, but then when I got to see Tommy and Kevin I was so glad to be with them. And they felt the same way. We all cried together for a long time. I think we needed that."

Katie groaned. "I know it is all working out, but he can't go pushing his way on everyone."

"I think he learned his lesson on that. You could talk to him about it and see what he says. If he acts like he's going to be pushy you could continue to punish him."

Katie looked quickly at Gwen, was she really punishing him? She didn't exactly want to punish him, just teach him not to lie to her.

Gwen shrugged, "Are we still doing inventory? Want me to just do the next section over from the toys?"

Katie nodded as she continued to think about Chase and her actions. She admired how pretty the bracelet looked on her wrist and knew she couldn't hold him off forever, but she still wasn't quite ready to see him. She did miss him, more than she wanted to admit, even to herself, especially to herself.

The glass people were coming tomorrow, maybe after that.

∼

As Chase worked on the ranch he worried about Katie and if he was reaching her. He only had a couple more ideas left to convince her that he wasn't the jerk he'd appeared to be. So, as he strung barbed wire, and checked on the hay and straw out drying in the hot sun, he wracked his brain for other possibilities. The town festival and rodeo was in a few weeks, he wanted Katie by his side at the dance and fireworks display.

His brother Adam snapped his fingers in his face. "Earth to Chase. What the hell are you thinking about?"

Chase debated telling him the truth. When he couldn't think of any other excuse, he did just that. "Katie."

"Not too big of a surprise I suppose. I've just never seen you so worked up over a woman."

"She's the one, Adam. She's my Rachel."

Adam nodded. "Ah, no wonder, I guess I had a few moments like you're having when I thought Rachel was leaving. At least Katie lives here and you can keep working on her."

"Not seeing her is driving me crazy."

"It's only been a few days, you didn't see her every day before."

Chase huffed out his frustration. "No but I *could* if I wanted to. I could walk into her store, or call her, or send her a text, any time I wanted."

"Her store is a place of business and open to the public, you still could go in there."

"Nope, not until I know she isn't going to look at me the way she did. She was so angry and disgusted with me, with a heavy dose of hurt and betrayal under it. I never want to see that expression on her face again." His gut twisted remembering her face and the words she'd said to him.

"But things are working out in the best possible way for Gwen and her brothers. If you hadn't interceded Gwen might still be on the streets and her brothers would not be getting the help they need. That's got to count for something."

"I sure hope so. I sent some things with Gwen today, so I'm hoping for a good report from her when she gets back. But I'm running out of ideas." His heart was so heavy in his chest, hopelessness weighed a ton.

Adam shrugged. "Well, when you run out of ideas, if she hasn't taken you back yet, we'll have a Kipling family powwow, and come up with some new ones. You and Cade know her the best, but the rest of us might have an idea or two that you wouldn't think of."

"Thanks, Adam."

Adam punched his shoulder. "Now let's get this work done, so you can go back and see what Gwen has to say."

"Sounds like a plan."

CHAPTER 29

The glass for her front window was finally arriving today. Katie felt like doing a happy dance, she was tired of the gloom in the front of the store due to the plywood. How could under two weeks seem so long?

A lot had happened in those not quite two weeks, she'd gone from friend to lover to ex with Chase. That particular path didn't seem quite finished and she had to wonder if they would go back to friends or lovers. Deciding to ignore that issue for the moment, she continued to think about all that had happened.

She'd practically adopted a pre-teen girl and realized she could use someone to help a few hours each day. She'd found she could afford it and if she got someone who she could train on the register, it would give her a bit more freedom during the day.

Last but not least, she'd finally won at cards. The last one made her grin and wonder if Chase had been distracted by her, or if her luck had changed. She wouldn't know until she played cards with them again. She did hope they could at least get back to friends, she missed going out to the ranch, or at least the freedom to know she could go out there any time.

The glass company arrived in the morning which made life just grand. She asked them to put the plywood on the side of her building, so she could do something with it later.

Gwen came in, just as they were pulling out the plywood. "It's so much brighter in here without the wood over the window. I'm so sorry that I broke your window. It was a mean thing to do."

"I understand. Just remember next time you're tempted to do something similar how it felt later."

Gwen nodded enthusiastically. "I will. I don't like being mean and I don't like feeling guilty afterwards."

"Then you've learned a lesson from it. I'll be happy to have the glass back though, it is so much brighter."

"What are you going to do with the wood? It's such a cute picture."

Katie smiled. "It is, and I want to put it up in my apartment. Even if Chase and I don't get back together, I want to keep it." She wasn't sure if it would soothe her or make her ache if they didn't work things out, but she had to keep the picture.

Gwen gaped at her. "Do you really think you won't get back together? I would feel really bad if the two of you can't work this all out."

"I just can't say for sure. He's being really sweet, but what if he does things in the future that he thinks is for the best and I don't agree?"

"This time he was right," Gwen said decisively.

"Yes, but that doesn't mean he will always be right."

The girl thought about that for a moment. "I suppose not. But isn't that what a relationship is all about? Learning to, you know, compromise?"

Katie sighed, why did this young girl have to be so wise. "Of course, it is."

"Haven't you too been friends forever? Has he ever done something like this before?"

"He's made decisions in the past without asking me, but he's never lied to me or pretended he agreed with me and did something completely different. That's probably why it hurt so much when he did it this time. That, and I was really trying to help you, and he took that away. I had all these horrible ideas that they would haul you off, or send you back to abusive parents, or something dire. He didn't know that wouldn't have happened. He just got lucky."

Gwen nodded. "I see what you mean, but I still think it would be sad if this ruined everything between you two."

Katie had to admit, if only to herself, that she thought it would be sad too. "Time will tell, now let's get busy in the back, away from the window, so that the glass people have the room they need."

At the end of the day when her night shift employee showed up Katie realized she was both surprised and a little disappointed she hadn't heard from Chase all day. She hadn't thought he would give up on her that easily. Then again maybe he'd been busy on the ranch, but he could have sent a note or something with Gwen if he'd really wanted too.

She sighed as she turned the corner of the building to go up her stairs to her apartment. She was half way up the stairs before she realized she hadn't seen the plywood from her window. But she figured they must have put it back behind the stairs, it would be more protected back there. Did she want to go back down and look? Not really, she would remember to check in the morning.

Unlocking the door and kicking off her shoes, she dropped her things on the kitchen table and walked into her living room, where she stopped dead in her tracks. On her wall was the plywood picture mounted in a huge frame that was a perfect foil to the drawing. It was obvious Chase had done it. Years ago, she'd given the twins a key, so someone would have an extra set. He'd hung the other pictures exactly where she'd told him she was planning to put them, when they'd talked about it, the night he'd stayed over.

So, he'd spent half the day, at least, fussing over her. There was another card in the corner of the picture. She smiled as she pulled it out of the envelope. On the front was Chase and Cade on their horses with her horse in the middle saddled, all of them slumped and sad in the pouring rain. Inside the sun was out and she was on her horse with them, all six of them smiling. The words said, "You are our sunshine, we miss you."

She smiled and realized he was very close to winning her back, but they still needed to talk.

CHASE LEAPED for his phone when he heard it chime with an incoming text. He'd been waiting impatiently to see if Katie would text him about the picture he'd hung in her apartment earlier today. Cade had helped him get it framed and carried up to her home. They'd been as quiet as possible, so it would be a surprise.

She'd been off work about an hour and he'd not heard a peep. Maybe she'd gone out to dinner before going home. He sighed. Or it could be she still didn't want to talk to him.

So, when the phone finally chimed he hoped it was her. He'd knocked it on the floor in his haste to get to it and it had slid under the bed. He got down on his hands and knees and pulled it out from under the bed. But when he unlocked it he saw a text from Gwen.

Gwen: My Aunt Mary is here! We are staying at the Singing

River ranch tonight to get to know each other. She would like you to join us for dinner tomorrow night at that Mexican restaurant at 6:30. OK?

Chase: Of course, I'll be happy to meet her. Good luck!

Gwen: Tks, see you tomorrow.

Chase sighed, hoping everything would work out with Gwen and her aunt. They were family, so he had high hopes. Her aunt must have dropped everything to arrive within forty-eight hours. It was only about a six-hour drive, but still that was a pretty quick trip considering she probably had to get off work, make plans for her family and all that.

He might not have heard from Katie, but it looked like things were working out for Gwen, and that gave him peace.

CHAPTER 30

*K*atie was eagerly awaiting Gwen's arrival at the store. The girl had texted her last night saying that her aunt had arrived, and they were getting to know each other. She'd said she would be by this afternoon to tell Katie everything. Katie had been awake half the night hoping everything was going well and the two of them would bond. She'd probably looked out the window a hundred times today to see if she could catch a glimpse of Gwen and her aunt. Customers had been rung up and helped, but as far as any other work being done today, nope, it just wasn't happening.

Gwen hopped in the door about three in the afternoon with the biggest smile Katie had ever seen on the girl's face. All the anxiety Katie had felt all day melted away and she felt a matching smile form on her own face.

"I take it you like your aunt."

Gwen rushed over to her and threw herself into Katie's arms. "She's wonderful. We talked all night and then when we finally got up after sleeping all morning, we had blueberry pancakes for lunch. Aunt Mary is a lot older than my parents were and has grown kids, but she said I'll fit right in with her grandchildren. She's got two granddaughters my age."

Gwen drew a breath and kept right on speaking. "They all live on a big cattle ranch just like Chase's family does and she said I can have a horse of my own. And when my brothers get out of jail she said they will come to live there, too. We talked to them a little while ago and they are both excited about that idea. Oh, I hope they don't have to stay in jail too long. It's going to be amazing."

Katie couldn't help catching some of the girl's enthusiasm as it poured all over her and the store, running across the floor like a river and dripping off the counters.

Before Katie could speak Gwen said, "And it's only a six-hour drive from here, so maybe you can come visit. Or we can drive over here sometimes to see you."

Katie was touched by the girl's desire to see her, but wondered how long that would last in her new life. "That's great, we can text back and forth, too."

"We can, isn't it all wonderful?" She grabbed Katie's hands and brought them up between them pulling Katie close.

Katie grinned. "It's super-duper wonderful. I'm so happy for you."

"I'm happy for me too. What time does your night guy come in? My aunt wants to take you to dinner, so she can meet you and we can celebrate. I thought if he came in soon, we could go upstairs and get all prettied up."

"I'll call him and see if he can come in early tonight."

Gwen clapped her hands and twirled around in glee.

They spent two hours getting all prettied up with finger-nail polish and makeup. Gwen talked Katie into wearing a dress, so they poured through her closet looking for the perfect outfit. Gwen insisted on one that was a bit sexier than she would have normally worn to have dinner with someone's aunt, but she let the girl have her way. She let Gwen wear one of her more sedate dresses that actually fit her better than it did Katie, so she told Gwen she could keep it.

Aunt Mary knocked on Katie's door at six twenty and they spent the next few minutes getting acquainted before they walked down the street toward the Mexican restaurant that Gwen loved.

≈

CHASE WALKED into the restaurant at six twenty, his whole family stressed punctuality, to the point of believing if you weren't ten minutes early you were late. So, he knew he would be there before Gwen and Aunt Mary. Which he realized was a good thing, because as soon as he walked in, memories of eating here with Katie assailed him. They'd had so much fun that night, that he felt a physical ache not knowing if he could ever get back to that closeness with her.

He was surprised when the hostess took him to the back room, it was usually reserved for big parties. But today it was setup with a single table. He wondered if Aunt Mary was trying to shield Gwen from prying eyes, so she had arranged a private area. That was a nice sentiment, but not really necessary, their town wasn't catty or mean.

He settled in and started thinking about what his next step should be in his campaign to win Katie back, when she walked in the door with Gwen and an older woman he assumed was Aunt Mary. When Katie saw him, she stopped dead in her tracks, but Aunt Mary and Gwen each took an arm and propelled her forward. His eyes drank her in, she looked amazing all dressed up with makeup on. He was certain if she'd been wearing a gunny sack with dirt on her face, he would have felt the same way.

He heard Aunt Mary say, "This was my idea, he had nothing to do with it." Which propelled him to leap to his feet to greet the woman and hold out chairs for all three women to sit. Katie ended up sitting next to him and as he pushed in her chair he breathed in the scent of her, she was wearing the perfume he'd bought her, which made his heart soar.

Gwen was on his other side with Aunt Mary across the table from him. She looked him up and down, which made him glad he'd worn his good jeans and boots and a nice western shirt with pearl snaps. Then she said to Gwen. "He doesn't look like an idiot, and he has very nice manners."

Katie looked at him with narrowed eyes. "He's not always an idiot, in fact most of the time he's a great guy. But when he is an idiot it's colossal in scope." He winced, and his heart plummeted at her cool tone of voice.

Gwen shrugged. "But it does work out for the best."

"I was only trying to help," he said in his own defense.

Aunt Mary spoke up again. "I very much appreciate the fact that you did act, Chase. Gwen might have gotten hurt living on the streets. Even in this quaint town, something bad could have happened. So, thank you for getting the Sheriff involved so they could contact me."

Aunt Mary turned to Katie. "I appreciate you taking care of her, and Gwen tells me you were trying to get her to tell you the truth, when Sir Galahad over there, burst in the door with the police and CPS. So, thank you for that, I wish you'd have confronted her earlier, but I understand that she might have just run off, if you tried before she trusted you."

She looked between the two of them. "Thank you so much for taking care of my girl, and also for knocking some sense into her brothers. I believe they got a very fine wakeup call, ending up in jail. Grief and uncertainty, with a large helping of booze made them a little on the crazy side. I think they'll learn from this, and toe the line when they get out. My husband and I plan to put them to work on the ranch." She looked at him again. "That should keep them busy, don't you think, young man?"

He grinned at her. "Yes ma'am, it surely will. Not much time for acting a fool on a cattle ranch, and if you do, the others will bring you back into line with a quickness."

The waitress brought in a pitcher of margaritas and a lemonade for Gwen. They gave her their orders and Katie poured the margaritas.

Aunt Mary took a drink from hers and then set it down and looked at him again. "Speaking of being a fool." He winced, and she looked back at Katie. "How long are you going to make this boy suffer? Gwen said he's done a fine job of apologizing and even some long distance groveling."

Katie just looked at him for a long minute and he could not read her at all, he had no idea what she was thinking, and his hands started to sweat. He was glad he'd already set his drink down, so he couldn't drop it.

Katie didn't say a word, she looked back to Aunt Mary and shrugged.

His heart plummeted to his feet and he felt like throwing up, she was never going to forgive him.

Aunt Mary wasn't giving up though, bless her. "You know I've been married to that man of mine longer than you've been alive, and the one thing I learned is that a man has to be told explicitly what it is we expect from them. What we need from them. Now I know you are a smart woman and you've figured out that what Chase actually did, was the correct course of action, and has been a positive thing all around. So, it's not what he did, but how he did it that's got your tail in a twist. Is this correct?"

Katie nodded, still saying nothing.

He opened his mouth, but Aunt Mary shook her head at him, so he closed it.

She said, "Now Katie, tell the poor stupid man what he should have done."

Katie frowned and looked at him. "All you had to do was talk to me. Explain what you thought was best. I might have argued, but I'm not an idiot. You didn't have to go behind my back, like I can't listen to a good idea and change my mind. You lied to me, you treated me like I was stupid. You let Drake and the CPS woman think I was unreasonable, and you made it look like I betrayed Gwen. And all you had to do was talk to me, dammit."

"Katie...."

She shook her head at him. "Why in the hell didn't you just talk to me? You've known me all my life and you didn't trust me enough to even talk about it."

His heart shattered at the pain he saw in her eyes as they filled with tears.

"No Katie, it wasn't like that."

"Then what was it like, Chase?"

He shrugged. "I was just protecting you."

"I don't need protection all the fucking time. I need a partner."

He flinched, Katie never used the f-word, she was really, really angry and hurt. And that destroyed him up. "Oh Katie. I'm so sorry, so damn sorry. I do want to be your partner."

The waitress came in with their food and Aunt Mary started talking. Chase had no idea what she was talking about because his mind was whirling with what Katie had said. He barely tasted his food and he and Katie didn't share bites like they had for years. His heart hurt. He didn't know how to fix it. He'd lost her, he'd lost his best friend and the only woman he wanted to spend his life with.

When dinner was finished Aunt Mary said, "Chase?"

"Yes, ma'am?"

Aunt Mary sighed. "What did Katie say she wanted?"

"For me to talk to her."

Aunt Mary lifted her eyebrows. "And what are you doing now?"

He looked at Katie who seemed to be as sad as he was. He glanced back at Aunt Mary. "Not talking, and trying to figure out how to fix it. If I even can fix it."

Aunt Mary narrowed her eyes. "You can't fix it."

His hopes plummeted even further.

She glanced at Katie and then back at him. "You can't fix it by yourself, Chase. But if you talk to Katie, the two of you can fix it."

He looked at Katie and she nodded so slightly he wasn't sure he'd seen it. But his heart knew and there was a tiny glimmer of hope. "Really?"

Katie nodded again a little bigger this time. He glanced at Aunt Mary and Gwen who were nodding too. His heart leapt.

He jumped up and took Katie's hand. Pulling her up and toward the door. Then he stopped, dropped her hand, turned and gave both Gwen and Aunt Mary a bone-crushing hug before rushing back to Katie. He called out over his shoulder, "Thanks for everything. I owe you both."

When they got outside he didn't know where to go to talk. He stood on the side walk looking up and down the street.

Katie laughed and pulled him toward the parking lot where his truck was. "You want to talk in my truck?"

"Anywhere is fine."

She got into his truck and he shut the door to hurry around to his side.

"What's this?" she asked when he got in.

"Something for later." He took the package and card out

188

of her hands and put it on the dashboard. "I really am sorry I made such a mess of all of this. I didn't think any of those things you said. I do trust you. I know you're not an idiot and are reasonable. I don't know why I didn't talk to you about it first. I won't ever do that again. This has been the worst few days of my entire life. It's like I can't draw a full breath. My heart hurts too much. I need you in my life, Katie. Please give me another chance."

She looked at him for a long minute while he held his breath. Finally, after what felt like a hundred hours, she nodded. "I'll give you another chance, but you are going to swear to talk to me about all important decisions, and even the unimportant ones."

The breath he'd been holding whooshed out of him. "I promise. I don't want another week like this one."

She rolled her eyes at him. "It's only been five days."

"Well, it felt like five weeks. Can I drive you home and maybe kiss you goodnight?"

"You can drive me home, then you can come up and give me your blood oath to communicate better. I think I'll make you sign a contract. Then you can kiss me goodnight."

"It's a deal."

When they got in her apartment he handed her the package and card. "Now you can open it."

She shrugged and pulled out the card which was another superman card about her being his kryptonite, she laughed and shook her head as she looked at it. Then she opened the gift. He'd gotten the idea for it when he'd been out thinking and checking the fence lines.

It was a heart made out of barbed wire, with a burlap bow and a twine hanger. But the most important part was a little wooden heart attached to the bow. Into the wood he'd burned their initials. He'd put all his hopes into that heart

189

with their initials, that someday they might be able to get back to loving each other, and she would want the gift.

She looked at it for a long time and he wondered what she was thinking. Slowly she ran her fingers over their initials. "This one took a lot of guts. What if I'd thrown it at your head?"

"Not guts. Hope. Tons and tons of hope. I love you Katie, and I don't want to spend my life without you. I know I have a lot of work to do to get back to where we were five days ago, but I'm willing to put in the time and the energy. I need you in my life. When you're ready, I want to ask you to be my wife."

She sucked in a breath and looked at him.

He put his fingers over her lips. "Don't say anything, yet. I know it's too soon. But I had to tell you that's my goal. What I plan to work toward. Every day. Every minute of every day, until you're ready."

He pulled her into his arms and kissed her softly, relishing every second. She sighed and melted into him, so he took the kiss deeper. She amped up the heat and wrapped herself around him. He reveled in her response and felt his heart solidify from the fragments it had become.

She pulled back. "I want to play cards."

He was certain all the blood had left his head and he hadn't understood what she said. "What?"

"I want to play poker."

He blinked at her and pulled back. "Um, okay."

He looked stupidly around the room, he didn't think she even had cards, let alone poker chips. "Do you have cards? And something to use for betting?"

"Cards? Maybe somewhere. And the betting will be articles of clothing." She gave him a wicked look.

"Clothing?"

She nodded. "Yes, I believe it's called strip poker."

He laughed a strangled laugh, as lust shot through him.

She shrugged one shoulder. "Or we can skip the cards, and just go straight to stripping."

He grinned, and his heart soared. "Katie, I will strip for you anytime, anywhere."

She put her hands on the sides of his shirt and tore it open, thank God for snaps on western shirts.

She grinned at him. "Good, start now."

The End

Made in the USA
Middletown, DE
27 May 2019